The Elusive Dud by Edgar Wallace

Richard Horatio Edgar Wallace was born on the 1st April 1875 in Greenwich, London. Leaving school at 12 because of truancy, by the age of fifteen he had experience; selling newspapers, as a worker in a rubber factory, as a shoe shop assistant, as a milk delivery boy and as a ship's cook.

By 1894 he was engaged but broke it off to join the Infantry being posted to South Africa. He also changed his name to Edgar Wallace which he took from Lew Wallace, the author of Ben-Hur.

In Cape Town in 1898 he met Rudyard Kipling and was inspired to begin writing. His first collection of ballads, The Mission that Failed! was enough of a success that in 1899 he paid his way out of the armed forces in order to turn to writing full time.

By 1904 he had completed his first thriller, The Four Just Men. Since nobody would publish it he resorted to setting up his own publishing company which he called Tallis Press.

In 1911 his Congolese stories were published in a collection called Sanders of the River, which became a bestseller. He also started his own racing papers, Bibury's and R. E. Walton's Weekly, eventually buying his own racehorses and losing thousands gambling. A life of exceptionally high income was also mirrored with exceptionally large spending and debts.

Wallace now began to take his career as a fiction writer more seriously, signing with Hodder and Stoughton in 1921. He was marketed as the 'King of Thrillers' and they gave him the trademark image of a trilby, a cigarette holder and a yellow Rolls Royce. He was truly prolific, capable not only of producing a 70,000 word novel in three days but of doing three novels in a row in such a manner. It was estimated that by 1928 one in four books being read was written by Wallace, for alongside his famous thrillers he wrote variously in other genres, including science fiction, non-fiction accounts of WWI which amounted to ten volumes and screen plays. Eventually he would reach the remarkable total of 170 novels, 18 stage plays and 957 short stories.

Wallace became chairman of the Press Club which to this day holds an annual Edgar Wallace Award, rewarding 'excellence in writing'.

Diagnosed with diabetes his health deteriorated and he soon entered a coma and died of his condition and double pneumonia on the 7th of February 1932 in North Maple Drive, Beverly Hills. He was buried near his home in England at Chalklands, Bourne End, in Buckinghamshire.

Index of Contents

CHAPTER I

THE PROFESSIONAL FRIEND

It was Felix Borcham who christened Archibald Dobbly "The Dud." Borcham's words were so many laws, and his appellations carried authority. His factories covered acres of ground on the outskirts of London, and his was the finest house in Brackton, that toney suburb.

In Brackton the social centre was the golf club, and it was one evening after a dance, when the men were gathered together in the smoke-room and conversation took a wide and personal range, that Borcham called Archie "Dob the Dud."

Dob looked a dud. There is something about an elegantly-dressed man which arouses the fiercest suspicions of his dowdy friends, and when a man carries his elegance to such lengths as did Archie, that suspicion is flavoured with contempt. Archie was fair, clean-shaven, and vacuous of countenance. He was the only man in Brackton who sported an eye-glass, and he had committed the crowning infamy of appearing at the golf dub in a shiny silk topper, white spats, and yellow gloves. What he did for a living, nobody knew. He had a tiny office in Queen Regent Street, which he attended punctually and regularly—he always went up to town by the 9.18 and travelled first-class—but what he did in that tiny office none knew.

It was some time after Brackton had accepted him as the kingpin of dudery that Dob revealed his guilty secret. The occasion was afternoon tea at the club one Sunday, and the boys had been chaffing him.

"What do I do, old thing?" he answered. "I do nothing."

"There are times when you look it," sneered Borcham, who was one of those tall, dark, good-looking men with a fine black silky moustache, and the habit of saying savage things in a matter-of-fact tone of voice.

"Possibly, possibly, dear old bird," replied Dob, waving his gloved hands, "but I had five years of doing things in France, old bean, perfectly horrible things. And I'm trying to get out of the habit."

Borcham flushed a deep red. During the period of war his services had been too valuable for the nation to dispense with in his capacity as managing director of Borcham's Manufacturing Company, Limited.

"Some of us were worth battalions of men at home," he almost snarled. "Personally, I volunteered six times, but the Ministry would not let me go."

"Hard luck, hard luck, old thing," murmured Dob. "It was much nicer in Brackton, I assure you. No," he went on, "I haven't quite decided what I am going to do. I've got a perfectly dinky little office and a jolly little typewriter that I'm learning to work, but I haven't decided whether I'll be a manufacturer's agent or a private detective."

There was a roar of laughter at this, but Dob did not join.

"Not so much a private detective as a worldly adviser to the young and innocent," he explained solemnly, and all within hearing of his voice shrieked with merriment. Borcham's guffaw was loudest.

"You'd make a jolly fine friend and mentor to people in trouble," he said sarcastically.

"I think I should," agreed Dob complacently.

"All right," sneered Borcham, "when I want a little advice I'll come to you."

Dob took a notebook from his pocket and solemnly wrote down Felix Borcham's name.

"I'll reckon you as my first client," he said.

He looked up suddenly and fixed May Constance with his steady grey eyes, which were by far the best of his features.

"And you shall be my second, Miss Constance."

The girl flushed, and those who were looking at her saw her lips tremble for a moment: then with a lift of her chin she rose and walked away. Borcham, with a savage look in Dob's direction, followed her.

A little silence followed this incident. Everybody knew that Dob had put his fool in it. There was nothing between Felix Borcham and May Constance. There was hardly likely to be anything "between" a man who was reputedly a millionaire and a girl who occupied a fairly humble position in his city office. He was not the kind of fellow who would marry for love. Felix had social ambitions, but he was nevertheless sweet on May Constance, whose father before his death had been a respected member of the club.

It was one of those attractions which make people feel a little uncomfortable, because not even the most sentimental imagined that Felix contemplated matrimony. There were ugly stories attached to his name, but since those stories were in the category of rumours and the club and its members knew nothing officially, Felix was received in the best houses and amongst the best people; for Brackton was not only a wealthy suburb, but numbered amongst its citizens a millionaire or two, an author or two, an Under-Secretary of State, and innumerable recipients of the honour of knighthood.

Those who know their London and its environs will not have any difficulty in placing Brackton on the map. Its beautiful houses facing the wide sweep of common long ago dedicated to the ancient volunteers, its historic windmill and its countrified atmosphere, despite its proximity to London, have made it famous the world over.

A week later, Kelby, the banker, had occasion to call upon Archie. Kelby was a young man for his position, and had a sneaking regard for the Dud. He had known him in the days of war, and the mud of the Flanders trenches cemented their acquaintance into friendship. He climbed up the two flights of stairs to the floor on which Archie's office was situated, and stood, paralysed, before the inscription upon the glass panel of his door.

ARCHIBALD DOBBLY.
CONFIDENTIAL ADVISER AND
PROFESSIONAL FRIEND.

read the notice.

"Good Lord, Archie," said Kelby, when he entered the diminutive apartment, "what's this game you're playing?"

Archie spun round in his chair, and his long knees almost barked against the opposite wall.

"Sit down, Kelby, old bird," he chuckled. "Yes. I've decided. That's my game."

"But, confidential adviser, Archie? Who's coming to you for advice?"

"Lots of people," answered Archie calmly.

"Rubbish, Archie," replied Kelby with a good-natured laugh. "You silly old owl! The moment your clients see your innocent face they'll fly."

The story was all over Brackton the same night. The Dud had started in business as a professional friend. When Archie made his appearance, as he did every evening, for a game of bridge, loud were the howls of joy which greeted him. Players at other tables with mock seriousness asked his advice on their hands and the calls.

Billy Sand, the club humourist, insisted upon a recipe for rheumatism, but through it all Archie never lost his sang froid. He was a grinning, cheerful young man when he left that night, though he knew the experience would be repeated on the following day. Of course, it died down after a week, and the club accepted Archie and his eccentricities as they accepted Felix Borcham with his unsavoury reputation.

Archie the Dud had not spoken to May Constance since that Sunday afternoon. Consequently he was a little surprised about a fortnight after his going into business, when she came out of the crowded dance-room and sank into a basket-chair on the verandah by his side.

"Aren't you dancing, Mr Dobbly?" she asked.

"No, Miss Constance," replied Archie: "it tires my old feet."

She laughed softly, and then suddenly became serious.

"I've heard about your new bureau," she said. "Is it a success?"

"It takes years to make a thing like that successful," evaded Archie.

"Do you have many clients?"

Archie coughed.

"Well, to be perfectly candid, Miss Constance, they haven't started rolling in yet."

She was silent for a while.

"Whom do you expect to get?" she asked.

Archie shrugged his shoulders.

"Do you know, Miss Constance," he said, very seriously for him, "this jolly old world is filled with people who've got a load of trouble on their shoulders, and who don't know where to turn to get advice. There are lots of people who don't want to go to doctors or to lawyers, and yet who dare not trust their own friends with their secrets."

She nodded.

"Sooner or later," Archie went on, "they are the birds who are coming my way."

"Do you think you can help them?" she inquired.

"Why not?" demanded Archie stoutly.

"But, have you the experience?"

Archie laughed, a low little laugh which surprised the girl, for she detected a note of confidence she had never suspected in this immaculate young man.

"Try me," he suggested softly, and she stiffened.

"Why should I try you?" she asked.

"When I said 'you' I meant the world," replied Archie calmly, but she was not to be put off.

"Do you think I want advice?"

"My dear young miss," explained Archie, "I'm a queer old bird. As you probably know, I usually come out from town very late every other night, which means that I spend my evenings in the West End. I never dine at the same restaurant twice, because I've always found that you get a view of the world, and an understanding of its follies by keeping out of ruts. Now, the other night I was dining at Billilis," he remarked carelessly, and he felt rather than heard her start. "It's not the nicest of places," he mused, as if talking to himself. "It's all right for men who want to see the seamy side, and it's all right for girls who know no other side of life, but Billilis, with its private rooms, is not the restaurant I should take a nice girl to."

"You saw me?" she inquired in a voice a little above a whisper, and Archie nodded. "And—and Mr Borcham?"

He nodded again.

"What did you think?" she asked defiantly.

"Dear Miss Constance," replied the dud, feeling for his cigarette case, "I thought Borcham was a blackguard, but that wasn't a new impression by any means."

"But what did you think of me?"

"I thought you wouldn't have gone there unless you had a very good reason."

She rose a little unsteadily to her feet.

"I'm going to be your first client," she said.

"I thought you would," Archie nodded. "My office hours are from 11 to 4."

"I will be with you to-morrow at half-past eleven," she concluded.

Before twelve o'clock on the Monday Dob the Dud was in possession of her complicated story. He listened in silence, that curious vacant expression on his face, staring at the wall, as, hesitatingly, almost painfully, she revealed her secret.

"Father left no money when he died," she told him. "I've had to bring up my two younger sisters, and it has been a pretty hard struggle. Mr Borcham was very kind. He gave me a position in his London office, and though the salary was small, he promised to give me extra work and an immediate rise. He told me that if he gave me more than the other girls, people would talk, and, understanding that point of view, I did not wish to be favoured any more than the others. About twelve months ago an old debt of my father's was brought to my notice. It was for £400. Of course, I could have declined payment, but I didn't want my father's name to be dragged in the mud, because this debt was one connected with a particularly unpleasant service."

She did not tell him what service it was, nor did he inquire.

"I was distracted and did not know which way to turn, until at last I plucked up courage and went to see Mr Borcham."

She hesitated again.

"I hate telling you all this, Mr Dobbly. In fact, a week ago, if anybody had told me that I should be pouring out my troubles to you, I should have laughed at them."

"Dob the Dud," muttered Archie, and she flushed.

"You've heard that name? I'm so sorry I made you recall it," she apologised.

"Not a bit," said Archie cheerfully, "I rather like it. It's one of the best reputations a man in my business can get. Go on. Miss Constance, you saw Felix Borcham? What did he say?"

"He was very kind," answered the girl, and still she hesitated. "He had been a little too kind, and had asked me out to dinner with him; but there was something so furtive about it, that I had declined."

"I suppose he had asked you not to tell anybody at Brackton," Archie suggested, and she looked at him in surprise.

"Yes, that is what I objected to. Well, anyway, I summoned up courage, and saw Mr Borcham. He was very nice about it. He said he could arrange for me to have the money, but in order that there should be no talk, he would not let me have the money himself, but would arrange with an acquaintance of his, who carried on business as a moneylender. Naturally, I demurred at this, but he told me there would be no fuss, and nobody would be any the wiser. All I had to do was to write to this firm, and they would advance the money."

"What was the name of the firm?" inquired Archie.

"Jeffsons, of Regent Street."

Archie scribbled down the name.

"I wrote to them." continued the girl, "and received in reply a form which I was asked to sign. This called for the repayment of £800—the sum I borrowed was £400—in twelve months but the accompanying letter said that this was merely a matter of form. I would only be asked to pay £400, and could take ten years to make the repayment."

"Have you got that letter?" asked Archie.

"Wait. I will tell you," the girl went on. "I signed the form and received the money by return of post. A week ago I had a letter from Jeffsons, calling for the immediate repayment of the whole sum, saying that I had not kept my agreement—in the agreement I signed, I promised to pay at the rate of £50 a month, which, of course, was impossible for me. I was in a panic when I received this notice, and looked up the letter which had accompanied the form."

"And which," remarked Archie, "would, of course, nullify or amend the agreement you signed."

There were tears in the girl's eyes.

"I couldn't find it anywhere," she said in despair.

"You couldn't find it?" repeated Archie thoughtfully. "Had it been stolen?"

"No, it had not been stolen, so far as I know. It was in the box. I keep all my papers in a steel box, one of my father's old boxes."

"Anyway, it was missing," said Archie. "Now, what happened after?"

"I saw Mr Borcham—that was when you saw me at that horrible restaurant. He insisted upon going there. There was a lot that happened there which I won't dwell upon," she added with a little shiver. "It was rather horrible!"

"I think I can guess," said Archie gently. "Mr Borcham is a little crude at times. Is he going to lend you the money, or exercise influence on his friends?"

She shook her head.

"Not unless—" She did not finish the sentence.

"I see," put in Archie. "Now, will you leave this matter in my hands for a day or two?" he pinched his chin thoughtfully. "Could I come in and see that box where you keep your letters? I'll call to-night."

She nodded.

"Jeffsons, eh?" said Archie. "Have you got a copy of their letter-head?"

"I have the letter they have just sent," she replied, "and a blank sheet of their notepaper. I think the money was wrapped in that when it came. It has 'with compliments' written at the bottom."

"I'll be with you at half-past nine tonight," he told her, as she rose. "There's a dance on at the club, and it will be a good opportunity."

At half-past nine he entered the pretty little cottage where May Constance kept house for her sisters. The children were working at their lessons in the dining-room, and May led him straight to her shabby little workroom.

"Here is the box." She produced such a battered old steel box as lawyers use for the storing of documents. There were only a few letters and memoranda within, which she took out and laid on the table.

"There's their last letter," she pointed out, "and here's the blank sheet 'with compliments,' but their covering letter, the one in which they told me I should not have to pay for years, with no interest at all, has disappeared. I had another search today."

"Is the box kept locked?" asked Archie.

She nodded.

"Nobody has access to it?"

She shook her head.

"You have no servants?"

"Only a woman who comes in once a day for an hour, but she's perfectly honest."

"You found no evidence of the house having been broken into?"

She shook her head again.

"May I take this letter? I want to see who Mr Jeffson is."

She handed him both sheets, and he left her with a sinking feeling at her heart that she had made a mistake in going to him. After the relief of telling her troubles was over, she realised how little encouragement he had given to her. It had been madness to consult him! He—Dob the Dud! She smiled bitterly at the remembrance of that nickname.

Three nights later Mr Felix Borcham sat in his palatial library at The Chase smoking a fragrant Havana and reading the evening newspaper. He was the picture of a man at peace with the world, when his footman announced a visitor.

"Mr Dobbly?" repeated Borcham with a frown. "What does he want? Show him in."

Dobbly came in. He was in his usual band-box condition. His evening coat was shaped as though he had been melted into it; his winged collar was of the latest fashion.

"Hello. Dob," said Borcham unpleasantly, "have you come to give me some confidential advice?"

"Just a little," replied Archie, with a grin. "May I sit down?"

Borcham nodded ungraciously to a chair.

"Have a cigar," he growled.

"I prefer a cigarette; cigars are too strong for my immature palate," responded Archie, lighting a cigarette.

"Well," asked Borcham.

"In re May Constance," began Archie coolly, and Borcham sprang to his feet with lowering brow.

"What do you mean?" he demanded harshly. "She hasn't been fool enough to consult a dud like you?"

"That's just what she has done," confirmed Archie, comfortably crossing his legs.

"Have you come to pay her debt?" sneered Borcham.

"No. I've come to get a full discharge of her debt from the unregistered partner of Jeffson."

"I'll see you damned first," said Borcham, and then remembering, "I am not a partner of Jeffson's. I just know them."

"You are a partner of Jeffson's—in fact, you are Jeffson. It's one of your many minor enterprises," explained Archie gently. "You have committed an offence in the eyes of the law by carrying on that business without registering yourself as a moneylender. Offence number two is the minor one of not inscribing your name on their letter-head. Offence number three," he ticked them off on his fingers, "is conspiracy."

"Conspiracy!" gasped Borcham, and Archie nodded,

"I hate using the word, dear old bean," he went, on, "but it's the only word that occurs to my dull mind. You send a letter to this unhappy girl, in the course of which you tell her that she need not pay the interest, and can repay the principal at her leisure."

"Let her produce the letter!" cried Borcham.

"I am producing it," replied Archie, and laid a sheet upon the table.

"It is not the original, so don't attempt to tear it up. It is a photograph, written in trick ink, which disappears and leaves no trace after three days. It was a very simple matter to restore the writing, both by photography and by treating your secret ink with hot milk."

Borcham stared at the photograph.

"I know nothing about it," he muttered sullenly, and Archie rose.

"Then I am sorry it is going to be a vulgar Police Court case," he said, making for the door.

"Here, wait a moment," shouted Borcham. "I'll give her the discharge, and she can get out of my business to-morrow."

"In which case you must add to your discharge a cheque for two years' salary in lieu of notice," dictated Archie. "You must also resign from the golf club, and write a rattling good character for Miss Constance."

Felix Borcham raved and swore, but in the end he signed and paid. A week later he left his work and went abroad for a prolonged stay, but what interested the golf club most was his resignation.

"Why on earth did Borcham go away?" asked Kelby.

"I advised him to," said the bland Archie. "Dear old thing, you seem to forget that I am a professional adviser."

CHAPTER II

THE RAJAH'S EMERALD

Clients had begun to trickle into the office of Mr Archibald Dobbly, who advertised himself in blatant style as a "Professional Friend and Confidential Adviser."

Some of these clients were profitable and interesting. Not a few were embarrassing. A proportion was lured into his tiny rooms by curiosity, and came out wishing they hadn't investigated, for Dob had the gift of biting sarcasm, which was very painful to his victims.

One afternoon a man came into the office who was entirely a stranger to Archie.

"Sit down," said Dob, fixing his eyeglass and staring solemnly at the newcomer.

"Before I tell you my business," began the stranger, "I want to ask you if you are the Mr Archibald Dobbly who had the taxicab accident last week."

Dob nodded. He had been lunching with an old friend of his father's, Captain Simmonds, who was the marine superintendent of the Westward Steamship Company, and they were driving to Euston from whence Captain Simmonds was leaving for Liverpool, when the taxi had swerved and crashed into a motor car. In consequence there had been some little publicity, and Dob's name had got into the newspapers.

"Yes, I am the veritable Archibald Dobbly," he replied with a smile.

"Excuse my asking," apologised the stranger gravely. "It was curiosity which prompted me, and has nothing whatever to do with the commission which I hope you will undertake. Though," he added thoughtfully, "it is curious that your companion was Captain Simmonds. It only shows how long is the arm of coincidence."

Archie was impressed.

"My name is Smart," the other went on. "Ferdinand George Smart."

Dob bowed slightly.

"I am not a Londoner, though I have frequently spent long periods in the Metropolis," explained Mr Smart. "My business is in Bukarest—a beautiful city, Mr Dobbly, I trust that on some future occasion I shall have the pleasure of showing you round."

"The pleasure will be mine," answered Dob, wondering what was coming next.

"I have, unfortunately, to go back to Bukarest," Mr Smart continued. "If that necessity had not arisen, I should not have consulted you concerning the guardianship of my niece, Miss Arabella Smart."

Dob scratched his chin.

"I might as well be quite frank with you," said Smart. "My niece, who is now on her way home from America, was engaged to be married to a young man of violent temperament, and exceedingly unpleasant reputation. Fortunately, we were able to break off this engagement, and Arabella was at the time considerably upset by what she thought was an act of heartless caprice on my part. She has since had reason to be very grateful for my interference."

Dob smiled.

"Unfortunately, although my niece is perfectly satisfied that she had been saved from a life which could not have been other than most unpleasant and depressing, the young man, who is of Latin origin and, therefore, passionate and unreasonable, has conceived against my niece the most unreasoning and bitter hatred. He has threatened to do her a very serious injury, and I have every reason to believe that he will try to carry out his threat."

Still Dob waited for the exact character of the commission.

"As I say, I have to return Bukarest at once," observed Mr Smart, "and I can't go until I have engaged somebody who will meet my niece on the boat—that is where the coincidence comes in, for she is returning by the Westward liner Ironic—and see her safely to Calais."

"Why only to Calais?" asked Dob.

"Because the young man, being a political offender, for whom a warrant has been issued in France, will not dare to land on the Continent." explained Mr Smart.

"Well," smiled Dob, "that's a most simple commission, and I shall most certainly undertake it."

"I will pay you a fee of one hundred guineas, and will allow you fifty guineas for expenses," stipulated Mr Smart, and Dob accepted.

The fee was highly satisfactory.

"You are, of course, taking a certain amount of risk," he remarked. "You do not know very much about me."

"I have heard about you," said Mr Smart truly. "Naturally I did not take this serious step without pursuing certain inquiries." Dob wondered if he had learnt his nickname, and, if he had, whether he would care to trust so delicate a mission to the hands of "Dob the Dud." He would have been interested to know that Mr Smart, had made thorough inquiries, and that the disparaging remarks which had been passed about Dob's intelligence had been the deciding factor in the choice.

Mr Smart took a little notebook out of his pocket and consulted its contents.

"The Ironic berths at Liverpool on Wednesday. That is the day after tomorrow, at three o'clock p.m. Do you think you could get a permit to go on board?"

"I'm certain of that," answered Dob confidently. "In fact, I could get on board without a permit."

"Then you're my man," decided Mr Smart. He went on to describe the young person he was to meet.

To help the recognition, he provided Dobbly with a cabinet photograph of a very pretty girl, smartly dressed.

"That is my niece," explained Mr Smart. "You will not find your task a very disagreeable one."

Dob agreed with him. When his visitor had left and he had settled himself to think over the interview, he reached the conclusion that there were worse jobs in the world than running the Bureau of a "Professional Friend."

On the Tuesday night he left for Liverpool, and spent the evening with his friend.

"I didn't expect to see you up here, Archie," exclaimed old Captain Simmonds, on greeting him.

Dob told him of the object of his visit.

"The Ironic, eh?" asked Captain Simmonds. "She arrives tomorrow afternoon. Who's the lady? A friend of yours?"

Dob had not disclosed the exact nature of his commission.

"No, she's not a friend, but she's a relation of a client of mine."

"I'll give you a permit to go on board," said the marine superintendent. "For some reason or other we have received a special order that nobody is to go on to the Ironic, so if you'd got permission from our head office, my boy, it would have been pretty useless to you. I am going on the river to meet her, and I'll take you with me, and that's not a privilege I'd offer to anybody."

At noon the next day Dob stood on the fore-deck of a stout little tug that was nosing its way through the turbulent yellow waters of the Mersey. Half a gale was blowing, and the entrance to the river was shrouded in rain mists, but they picked up the hulk of the Ironic. She was laying at anchor, waiting for the river pilot, and the two tugs came up together.

A suit of oilskins, provided by the marine superintendent, had transferred Dob into something that looked like a sailor, and clambering up the rope ladder behind his old friend, he found the experience a little terrifying.

One of the ship's officials stood by the gangway.

"Who is this?" he asked sharply.

"Oh, that's one of my men," answered Captain Simmonds. "I'm going to the captain's office," he told Dob. "If you want me, I'll be there. You had better find your friend."

They had come aboard on E Deck, and slipping off his wet oilskins, Dob climbed the companion-way to the promenade deck above. Almost the first person he saw when he emerged on to the promenade was the girl he was seeking. She wore a beautiful sable coat. She was sitting on a deck chair, a rug over her legs, a sable wrap about her shoulders. He lifted his hat.

"Miss Smart, I believe."

She looked at him.

"Oh, you are the gentleman my uncle sent," she cried pleasantly, and pulled an empty chair towards her. "Sit down. Mr—"

"Dobbly is my name," Dob informed her, beginning to talk of the voyage.

He was conscious that the atmosphere of the ship was strained. The serious-faced Steward, the little knots of passengers gathered about the deck talking solemnly, all suggested that there was some kind of trouble on board the ship. He remembered what Captain Simmonds had said—that special orders had been given that nobody was to board the Ironic.

"Why is everybody so glum?" asked Dob, and she smiled.

"Oh, I suppose it is the loss of the Rajah's emerald that is worrying them."

"The Rajah's emerald?" repeated Dob in surprise.

"We've got a real live Rajah on board. The Rajah of Bimpore has, or had, the largest emerald in the world, worth tens of thousands of pounds. It disappeared from his cabin two or three nights ago, and they have been searching everywhere for it."

Dob whistled.

"But that oughtn't to make the passengers glum."

"It isn't that," the girl told him, "but on an occasion like this everybody is suspected. They're going to search all the passengers as they leave."

At that moment Captain Simmonds came along, his brows set in a frown. He beckoned Dob aside.

"I'm afraid I've committed an awful indiscretion getting you on board," he began. "We'll have to leave before the ship stops. She comes to a stop opposite the landing-stage, and a small army of detectives are coming on board to search for a confounded jewel that has been lost on the way. You'll have to come ashore with me on the tug. Will you meet me downstairs in five minutes?"

Dob said he would, and went back to the girl.

"I'm afraid I shall not be able to see you until you land, but I'll be waiting at the foot of the gangway for you."

"Will you send a telegram for me as soon as you get ashore?" she asked.

"Certainly," answered Dob. "Don't you think—"

Before he could speak, the girl had walked along the deck and had disappeared through the companion way. She came back in three minutes with a telegraph form.

"I've only American money," she remarked.

"Oh, I'll pay for the telegram," laughed Dob. "Now I am afraid I must go."

She walked with him downstairs and helped him into his oilskins, which he was carrying on his arm. A few minutes later he had made the perilous descent by the rope ladder and was steaming away, waving his hand to the girl as she leant over the side of the high deck above him.

He reached the dock, and stood by the side of the marine superintendent, watching the big boat in mid-stream.

"It'll be hours before she docks," said the latter. "You had better go along and come back at seven o'clock."

The rain was falling heavily. Dob buttoned up the collar of his overcoat, which he had worn under the oilskins, and trudged through the bleak approaches of the Liverpool docks on his way to the hotel. There was no cab in sight, and the waiting tram had no temptation for him.

He was halfway along a quiet street consisting of warehouses, when a man brushed past him, walking in the same direction.

Now Dob had not only a remarkable memory for faces, but a mental register of uncanny accuracy of figures. There was something about the man's walk which interested him, more than the fact that he had jolted violently against him, without so much as an apology.

Dob was quickly abreast of the man, and dropped his hand on his arm.

"Why, Mr Smart," he cried, in unfeigned surprise.

The man looked round at him.

"Mr Dobbly!" he exclaimed. His astonishment was less genuine.

"I thought you had gone away to Bukarest?" Dob asked him.

"I managed to break my engagement and stay on. I intended telling you, but I thought that two people could protect my little girl against the machinations of this villain better than one."

"You were on the landing stage when I come ashore, weren't you?"

Mr Smart hesitated.

"Yes, I was. I am annoyed to find that the ship won't be in for another four hours."

Dob related his experience of the afternoon.

"It's a great nuisance," said Mr Smart, though he did not seem to be particularly put about. "Just imagine the feelings of these perfectly innocent people who have to submit to the indignity of the search, Mr Dobbly. Won't you have a cup of tea?"

He paused outside a restaurant. Just then a cup of tea was very acceptable to Dob, so he followed his companion into the crowded tearoom.

"Why, you've cut your hand," cried Dob suddenly, looking at the other. The man's hand was roughly bandaged with a white handkerchief.

"I tore it on a nail a quarter-of-an-hour ago," Smart explained indifferently. "Some fool had been repairing the handrail of the little bridge leading to the landing stage, and, unfortunately, I hadn't my gloves on." Dob nodded. He, curiously enough, had seen the bungled job.

"It has been bleeding rather freely," continued the man, tightening the handkerchief. "It is rather ugly. I'll keep it out of sight."

Throughout the tea he talked about his niece and her disgruntled lover. He spoke affectionately, but sadly, of her distress when she learnt that the match had been broken off. Dob listened with interest, until he had occasion to rise to find a packet of cigarettes that he had slipped into his overcoat pocket that morning. As he took his hand from his overcoat pocket he saw something that brought an exclamation of surprise to his lips. Along the back of his hand appeared a red streak which was undoubtedly blood.

He glanced round at his companion, who was at that moment lighting a cigar, his attention directed elsewhere.

Carefully Dob pulled out the lining of his overcoat pocket; he had had it made of chamois leather, and there was a little patch of blood halfway down. Somebody had pushed his hand into that pocket and that somebody was Mr Smart. When could it have happened? Then Dob remembered. Smart had jostled against him in the street. At that moment his hand must have felt the pocket. Dob rubbed the stain from the back of his hand and went back to his chair.

"I think, Mr Dobbly, when this boat comes to the stage, I will take charge of my niece and save you any further bother."

Dob smiled slightly.

"I have been paid a very handsome fee," he murmured softly, "and I should like to earn it."

"As to the fee," the generous Mr Smart waved his bandaged hand, "we will talk no more about that. You have done your work, and there is no need to trouble you any more. I can tackle Antonio if he comes across our path. As a matter of fact," he added, "I have reason to believe that Antonio is in Scotland."

"Two can tackle him better than one," replied Dob. He beckoned the waitress.

"Give me my bill, please."

When it was brought he assisted Mr Smart on with his overcoat.

His plans had yet to be made, but as he took the overcoat from the hook, he saw a notice on the wall. It was a short printed notice issued by the proprietors of the restaurant offering a reward for the conviction of the thieves who were systematically robbing the restaurant of its cutlery. There were three metal spoons and a knife on the table. Surreptitiously Dob gathered them together in his hand and slipped them into Mr Smart's overcoat pocket. Dob walked to the pay desk, and put down half-a-crown, whilst his companion walked to the door and stood waiting in the street outside.

"Is that the manager there?" asked Dob, pointing to a man evidently in charge of the establishment.

"Yes, sir."

Dob walked to the man quickly.

"You're the manager, aren't you?"

"Yes, sir."

"Well, that fellow who is standing in the doorway, the man in the blue overcoat, has a few knives and spoons of yours in his pocket," said Dob. "I hate giving a man away," he added virtuously, "but this sort of thing ought to be stopped."

The manager ran to the door and opened it, and at that moment, as luck would have it, a policeman passed. With a jerk of his head the manager attracted him, and then he turned to the unconscious Smart.

"Excuse me, sir," he spoke severely. "I think you have some property of ours."

"Property of yours?" replied Smart, glaring at him. "What the devil do you mean?"

"You have some of our plate in your pocket."

"Rubbish!"

Smart put his hand in his pocket.

A look of comic amazement spread over his saturnine face as he drew out the spoons and the knife.

"How did they get there?" he stammered.

"That's a nice question to ask," said the policeman. "Do you charge this man?"

"I certainly charge him," cried the manager. "We lost four hundred pounds worth of plate last year, and I'm going to make an example of this man."

The policeman's hand fell upon Smart's arm, but with a twist the man wrenched himself free and ran.

They were after him in a second. He sprang on to the running hoard of a taxi, and this time he was no longer the gentle philosopher. There was a revolver in his hand.

"Drive on! If you stop I'll shoot you stone dead!"

The frightened driver accelerated, but by this time all Liverpool seemed to be aware that a man was making his escape from justice. As they swung round the corner of the street a policeman leapt on to the running board, and three minutes later, Mr Smart, handcuffed and firmly held, was on his way to the station, cursing volubly in three languages, for he had an international education.

When they searched him at the station they found no spoons or knives, but in a neat little package the emerald of the Rajah of Bimpore, the emerald which the girl had slipped into Dob's jacket on the ship, and which her confederate had taken from his pocket in the street.

"The whole thing was probably arranged by wireless," explained the superintendent of police, when Dob recounted the part he had played, "or maybe it was arranged for months ahead. These international crooks are pretty clever strategists. They employed you, thinking you were a mug, and possibly the fact that you were a friend of the marine superintendent's came to their knowledge. Smart's real name is Markar, and Miss Arabella Smart is known as 'Flash Emma' in continental police circles."

He looked at Dob admiringly and shook his head.

"I can't understand why they picked on you, for you've done a bit of the smartest detective work I've ever heard about."

"Possibly they thought I was a dud," replied Dob pleasantly, and the policeman smiled as though such a suggestion was too preposterous to entertain.

CHAPTER III

THE SHY MR BARKS

Mr Archibald Dobbly was the last person in the world that one would have expected Minnie Potter to consult in the matter of an affair of the heart. Minnie, who was thirty-five, was rather thin, angular, a little acidulated, and the main tenet of her faith was that if you put the worst construction upon any human action you are generally right.

Nobody had ever asked for Minnie's hand; either of them. She had never been wooed in the strict sense of the term, though many people had danced with her at the club, and quite a number of young men had driven her home. They had, with commendable caution, taken a third person with them to act as chaperone.

In consequence, Minnie Potter had reached the age of discretion without experiencing any youthful romance, and it would have taken a hurricane to convince her neighbours that she was in any way flighty.

Then came Willie Barks. He moved into Brackton from a garden city in the Midlands. He was thin, with long hair and baggy knickerbockers, and painted bad pictures. Probably amongst the many citizens of Brackton there was not a more inoffensive and unprotected male.

"Willie never barks nor bites," said Solomon Mendoz, the humourist of the club. "Give him a bone and a dish of milk, and he wants nothing more."

It was Mr Barks' ill-fortune that he chose a tiny detached cottage adjoining the somewhat pretentious house which was occupied by Ben Potter and his daughter Minnie.

The moment Minnie saw Willie painting in his garden, she thought it possible that at last here was a man who was destined to change the whole colour and hue of her existence. Later, when she made investigations, she was sure. Willie did not know this, for he stayed on in Brackton.

Dob the Dud, although a neighbour, knew nothing of the extraordinary influence which Willie Barks had produced upon the heart of Minnie Potter.

Dob went daily to his office to find an increasing volume of business to be dealt with. As "confidential friend and adviser," his clients had been few and far between, but he had acquired two or three colonial agencies, which were not only lucrative but interesting.

He had ceased to look for adventurous confidences and was seriously considering the painting out of the sign on his door. Consequently the advent of Miss Potter cane in the nature of a surprise and, since he knew her, something of a shock.

She was not unpleasant looking. There was a certain prettiness about her sharp feature, which might have been attractive but for the discontented droop of her mouth.

"Good morning, Miss Potter, this is an unexpected pleasure," said Dob, getting up and placing a chair for her.

Miss Potter was at some loss as to how she would begin. In truth, here was an embarrassing commission.

"The fact is, Mr Dobbly," she began, "I want to consult you on a very delicate matter."

Dob nodded. It was not the first delicate commission he had received, but he wondered exactly what business this shrewish little lady could have.

"Do you know Mr Barks?" she asked. "He has been in Brackton for two months."

"I know Mr Willie Barks by sight," replied Dob.

Miss Potter coughed.

"He in our next door neighbour," she explained, "and I have seen a great deal of him lately. We have had little conversations over the fence. He is a very shy man."

"Very," agreed Dob, amid there was another awkward pause.

"Now, Mr Dobbly, I am going to say to you what I would not say to anybody else," went on the young woman, speaking rapidly. "As you know, I am fairly well off, and so is Mr Barks. I am getting on in life and I have decided to get married. It isn't that I haven't had offers," she hurriedly explained, "but I have never felt that the man was quite worthy of me."

"That I can well understand," answerer Dob gravely. "Has Mr Barks the felicity of being—"

She shook her head.

"Mr Barks has said nothing, but I have seen an expression in his eyes, and I know that it is only his modesty which prevents him speaking. Now, Mr Barks has few friends in Brackton. If he had more I could have dropped a hint that there is no need for Willie to be afraid of asking me."

Dob was staggered. He could, and would have collapsed but for his innate sense of politeness. Of all the commissions he expected, the last in the world was that of matchmaker.

"I know it's immodest and horrible of me," Minnie went on, "but, really, Mr Dobbly, it would be ridiculous, and ever tragic, if Mr Barks lost the woman he desired, from sheer false modesty on my part."

"But what am I to do, Miss Potter? Do you want an introduction?"

"No, of course, not," she almost snapped. "I know Mr Barks very well. What I want you to do is to see more of him—take him out to dinner. Of course, you can send the bill to me."

Dob inclined his head. He was trying very hard not to laugh.

"And you can drop a hint to him—you understand? You're a man of the world."

"Exactly." said Dob. "I am a man of the world. Do you know anything of Mr Barks except that he wears his fair long, and is given to painting?"

"He belongs to a very good Cheshire family, I'm told," answered the girl, unconscious of the fact that her hearer was laughing inwardly, "and he would be in every way a desirable match. Will you accept the commission?"

Dob hesitated for a moment.

"Well—I—er—suppose so. It's an unusual job, but then most of my work is a little out of the ordinary. I'll see Mr Barks to-night."

"Of course, you'll not tell—you'll not let him know?"

"Secrecy is the basis of my business," he replied glibly.

When she had left he sat down to consider the problem. The more he thought the more absurdly grotesque it seemed. He did not know Barks, except that he was an inoffensive member of society who loved to parade the streets on Sunday morning, smoking a large pipe and wearing his ridiculous baggy knickerbockers. People liked him. One or two of the leading lights of Brackton society had invited him to dinner, and he was a visitor at a few of the houses. His paintings, so far as Dob could judge, were fair, but by no means out of the ordinary.

Dob did not know him very well, so he took the very first opportunity of enlarging his acquaintance. He found Mr Barks sitting in the deserted lounge at the club, playing a solitary game of patience. Willie looked a little apprehensive as Dob approached him.

"All alone, Mr Barks?" inquired Dob, good-naturedly.

"Yes er—yes," admitted Willie, with an air that suggested that he would prefer to continue in his solitary state.

Dob, however, was not to be denied. He sat down on the settee by the side of the little man, and such was his charm and his persuasive powers, that in a very short time he had Willie Barks talking earnestly and lucidly about Willie Barks.

Dob called to mind all the artist talk he had ever heard, and worked it off on his victim.

"Not much to paint here, Mr Barks," he remarked. "Have you ever tried Dartmoor? There is colour and—"

"Dartmoor!" almost screamed the little man. "Nonsense! Rubbish! It's an ugly place—a dirty, creepy place—ugh!"

Promptly he grew calmer mud returned to his favourite topic, which was himself.

"I'm not very keen on company," he admitted. "Women, of course, scare me to death. You see, Mr Dobbly, I am rather a misogynist."

"But surely you won't remain a misogynist all your life?" asked Dob.

"I think I shall," answered Mr Willie Barks, nodding rigorously. He had a tiny little beard, that wagged comically on his chin as he nodded. "Oh, yes, I think I shall. I shall never get married—never!"

"But there must be lots of nice girls whom you could make happy," observed Dob revelling in his role of match-maker.

"I think not," said Willie, shaking his head just as vigorously. "No, I don't think so, Mr Dobbly. The very sight of girls frightens me. There's a young lady who lives in the next house from mine, a very nice girl—"

"By the way, are you short-sighted?" asked Dob innocently.

"No: why do you ask?" demanded the astonished Mr Barks.

"Nothing—go on."

"I was saying there's a very nice girl who lives next door to me. Sometimes she peeps over the fence, and it is just agony to me, especially if I am sitting painting and cannot make my escape. Once she tried to attract my attention. I feel sure she means well, but if—" He looked inquiringly at Dob, a light shining in his eyes. "Do you know the young lady—Miss Potter, I think it is?"

"I do." replied Dob, enjoying himself.

Mr Barks looked round to discover if he could be overheard, and dropped his voice.

"Perhaps you would drop a hint to her, and ask her most kindly not to look over the fence whilst I'm painting. It causes me most acute mental agony."

Here, thought Dob, his commission ended, for obviously here were two irreconcilable factors.

He reported progress to Minnie Potter, who scoffed at him.

"Really, Mr Dobbly, you had an excellent opportunity for saying what I wished you to say, but you didn't seem to avail yourself of it."

"If I had," retaliated Dob, "he would have certainly run away, and you would never have seen him again."

Minnie Potter bit her lip thoughtfully.

"The man is a genius," she mused, more to herself, than to Dob. "You've no idea how he is neglected. He has a girl in every day to clean the house for him, but he's only in two hours—what can she do? All the rest of the time he is quite alone. He never asks people in to see him, and he cooks his own meals. It is dreadful that a man of his high mentality should be allowed to ruin his digestion. It is a mistaken kindness to humour his eccentric wishes, Mr Dobbly."

The next day, when Willie Barks came into his garden, he discovered a large basket which had been carefully lowered over the garden fence—there was a piece of cord still attached to the handle. Under a snowy napkin lay a variety of tempting dishes. Willie took one glance at them, and fled back to the house. He was not seen again for two days.

Dob saw him on the third day going to town, dressed in a black Inverness coat and carrying a big portfolio under his arm. He made a curious figure.

Apparently he was something of an etcher, and Dob, passing his house and seeing a light burning in his window at two o'clock in the morning, guessed that the little man was grinding out his art.

There were features of his commission which puzzled Dob. In the first place, it was unlike Minnie Potter to fall violently in love with anybody. In the second place, her father was not in a financial position to support an artistic son-in-law.

Ben Potter, so far from being well off, as Minnie had claimed, was at the moment wading through a sea of writs. It was fairly well known that both he and his daughter had a very keen eye for the main chance. Miss Potter had also a reputation for taking too intense an interest in other people's business. There was a scandalous story of her having intercepted and opened, letters of a lady who was a guest at the Potters' house, whilst her own home was being disinfected after a visitation of measles.

Dob grew more interested, not in the task which had been given him, but in the character of his client. Hitherto, he had not paid very much attention to the Potters, who were not amongst the most popular people in Brackton, but he was led to make a call upon the lady who had complained of Miss Potter's inquisitiveness.

"It is perfectly true," averred that indignant housewife. "Minnie opened all the letters that came. I caught her steaming them over a kettle. Of course, I left the house immediately, and went to the station hotel. But she has always been like that."

A light was beginning to dawn on Dob.

Willie Barks' home was next door to the Potters', and it would have been very easy for Minnie to obtain access to that house whilst the little man was away selling his sketches—if he ever did sell them—in London.

Dob sat that night in his room, piecing together the facts as he knew them. First and foremost he decided that Minnie was not in love with Willie Barks, but had a very special and particular reason for wanting to marry him. Therefore, knowing Minnie's character, it must be that she wanted not so much a husband as a bank account. This was the puzzling feature of the case, because Willie was apparently as poor as a church mouse. He made no secret of the fact that he had no income beyond a few pounds a week, left to him by a maternal aunt, and the proceeds of the sale of his pictures, which Dob judged to be practically nothing.

He went to see Minnie Potter, and arrived so unexpectedly that the young lady thought he had exceptional news to tell her. She was disappointed and annoyed when she discovered that the only object of his visit was to question her about Willie Banks' financial position.

"I don't care how poor he is," she said so emphatically that, for a moment, Dob was deceived. "He may be on the verge of bankruptcy, or be may be a miser. It makes no difference me."

"But how would you like to live in that small house, Miss Potter?"

"Good gracious," she answered, betraying herself for a second by her scorn, "do you imagine I'd live in a tiny little place like that with only three rooms and an attic? If I did I'd want the place put into a thorough condition of repair. The papers on the walls are—" She stopped in some confusion, seeing Dob'a eyes fixed on her.

"How do you know? Have you been in the house?" he asked quietly.

"Yes—no," she replied. "Well, to tell you the truth, Mr Dobbly, I did look in one day when Mr Barks was in town. I know it was naughty of me, but I was lust frantic with curiosity about him. You can guess just how a girl feels about a man she is fond of."

"I can guess," remarked Dob drily. "So you went into the house?"

"Our key fits his door," she explained, without shame. "I just wanted a peep."

"Well," inquired Dob, "how much money did you discover?"

She went a deep red.

"Money?" she stammered. "What do you mean?"

"Did you find that Mr Willie Barks was very well off indeed?"

She looked at him sharply.

"Did you know that, too?" she asked quickly. "Did he tell you?"

Dob shook his head.

"No, I guessed. Tell me all about it, Miss Potter."

But it was some time before she was prepared to give him a narrative that bore any resemblance to the truth. As far as Dob could gather from her scattered explanation, interspersed as it was with excuses for her own dishonourable conduct, she had gone into the house one day and had made her way up to Mr Barks' bedroom.

"Of course, the furniture is the cheapest stuff you could imagine," she continued contemptuously. "I should alter all that, however, if—Well, as I was going to say, I turned down the coverlet of the bed to see what sort of linen he used. Just imagine my surprise, Mr Dobbly, to discover that the bed was covered with one pound notes. There must have been twenty thousand of them if there was one! You would never think a little man like that would be a hoarder of money, would you?"

Dob was silent.

The vision of Willie Barks, with his long hair, his tiny beard, and his knickerbocker suit, rose before him. He remembered Mr Barks' sudden agitation when he suggested that he should paint the beauties of Dartmoor.

"New money?" asked Dob slowly.

"Yes, straight from the bank," answered Minnie, with pardonable enthusiasm.

Dob cut short his visit abruptly, and an hour later he was in town. He drove straight to Scotland Yard, and told the Chief Commissioner of the Criminal Investigation Department on the point of leaving.

Without considering Miss Minnie Potter's fine feelings, he told the Chief Commissioner all he knew about Willie Barks.

"Painting, of course, was an excuse for engraving and I rather fancy that Willie Barks' long suit is in the latter department."

"I agree with you," replied the Commissioner thoughtfully. "We have had a tremendous number of forged Bradburys put into circulation lately, and we have been trying our best to get at the forger. Come along with me to the Record Department."

The Record Department was the most business-like Government department Dob had ever been in. In the county gaols the portraits of prisoners are arrayed, irrespective of their offences, their ages, or their peculiar characteristics. At Scotland Yard they are cross-indexed, so that peculiar types of criminals can be discovered immediately.

Half-way through a big fat book labelled "Forgers," Dob discovered Mr Willie Barks. It is true that his hair was shorter, that he was innocent of beard, and his name was described as William Tanner, but it was Willie sure enough.

Beneath was written a list of his convictions, and this significant biographical note—

"Has a taste for painting, and is usually to be found in an artistic set. He poses as being shy but has been twice married, bigamously."

"That's Willie," vouched Dob grimly.

Accompanied by two detectives, he returned to Brackton, but just a trifle too late.

That afternoon, whilst he was interviewing the Chief Commissioner, Miss Minnie Potter had put two and two together, and had interviewed Willie.

"So you discovered all that money, did you?" said Willie with extraordinary sharpness for one who was so diffident and reserved, "and you told that infernal dud, Dobbly."

"Why, of course, Mr Barks. You see," she responded, "Mr Dobbly was working for me."

"And he's gone to town!" mused Willie.

"Yes, Mr Barks."

"Well, I think I had better go to town, too. If I don't come back, Miss Potter—"

"Yes?" she asked expectantly.

"You can have all the money you find in my house. There is nearly a hundred thousand pound, and I hope you will put it to a very good use. In fact, nothing would please me better than if you gave it to Dob," added Willie.

"I shall certainly not do that," replied Minnie. "Of course, I can't accept—"

But Willie Barks was gone. He did not go to town. In fact, competent witnesses say that the train he took went in the opposite direction.

When the whole truth was revealed, Minnie turned like a fury upon Dob.

"I didn't engage you to drive him away," she stormed. "He is probably more sinned against, than sinning."

"That is what his other wives think," said Dob simply.

CHAPTER IV

A DEAL IN ECFONTEINS

Mr Ebenezer Jackson held tight to one faith. It was, that there was a fool born every minute. Working on this simple formula, Mr Jackson had built up a respectable bank balance, had acquired an estate in the country, and was a member of two golf and three racing clubs.

Between ten o'clock in the morning and five o'clock in the afternoon, Mr Jackson was a stock jobber. He bought and sold shares for the most complacent, and at the same time, the most exacting of clients. In other words, he dealt in them for himself.

Men who deal in any particular commodity, whether it is furniture or china, postage stamps or antiques, frequently find themselves the possessors of a great deal of picturesque but unsaleable stock. They also discover at intervals that what has been sold to them as a genuine article, does not, on examination, bear the hall mark of genuineness.

In the course of his long and profitable career, Ebenezer Jackson had accumulated quite a pile of fairly useless stock. The hundred thousand shares in the Ecfontein Coal Mine of South Africa had cost him a little less than a shilling a share. But they were dear at the price, and later Mr Jackson would have gladly sold them at sixpence or even threepence. As it was, they represented to him a dead loss of five thousand pounds, and when Ebenezer Jackson had a loss, it hurt him worse than toothache.

For years, on one pretext or another, he had endeavoured to palm off his hundred thousand shares upon his unsuspecting friends. Unfortunately for him, he had never found a friend sufficiently unsuspecting. They had listened to his stories of the wonderful possibilities of Ecfontein Collieries with polite but sceptical interest.

He was a bachelor and lived in one of the biggest houses in Brackton with his niece. His bank balance was an amazing one, and yet the thought of those five thousand pounds spent on Ecfontein Collieries had rankled in his mind for thirty years.

Ecfontein Collieries were chiefly remarkable for the fact that they contained little or no coal. They were too far away from the main reef for Mr Jackson to offer them as gold shares, and he had reluctantly given them up as a bad job when the fame of Archibald Dobbly came to him, and his hopes revived.

Dob, returning to Brackton after a hard day's work in the city, was surprised to find waiting for him an invitation to dinner from Ebenezer Jackson. They had met once or twice at the golf club, where Jackson had shown not the slightest desire for any better acquaintance with Dob the Dud.

"Another client," murmured Dob. He would have been surprised if he had known that Mr Ebenezer Jackson regarded him in the same light.

On the afternoon when the dinner was to be celebrated, Mr Ebenezer Jackson returned home early, and interviewed his niece. She was about twenty-five, pretty, with a dark complexion, and was rather over-ruled by the superior knowledge of her sophisticated uncle.

"Now you understand, Mona, I don't want you to come in to dinner. You had better go to your Aunt Rachael's, and at a quarter past nine I want you to ring me up on the telephone and say what I tell you to say. You will find it written down here."

He handed her a paper, which Mona Jackson read with interest.

"I am determined to get rid of those infernal colliery shares," continued her uncle, "and I think that this is the best opportunity we have had. This fellow Dobbly is adventurous, and has plenty of money. I rather fancy that we shall make a killing which will enable me to purchase that imitation beaver coat which you have been asking for."

"It is a beaver coat, not an imitation," said Miss Jackson severely.

"I will even buy a real beaver coat, though it's an absurd waste of money, when a good blanket coat will keep you just as warm."

Dobbly arrived five minutes before the appointed time, and found Mr Ebenezer Jackson waiting for him in the old-fashioned mahogany drawing-room.

The fates fought for Dob that night. On the way up from his house, remembering that he had not bought an evening newspaper, he had taken one at the street corner opposite the railway station, and had thrust it into his pocket.

Fate willed that his host, after a cordial greeting, should be seized with a fit of sneezing, and should discover that he had not a pocket handkerchief. This necessitated his leaving the room for about five minutes, during which Dob whiled away the time by glancing at the newspaper.

There was one paragraph which caught his eye:—

"The South-Eastern Cable Company announces that, owing to a submarine disturbance, the cable has been fractured, and the South African service is liable to three or four days' delay."

Dob put the paper out of sight on Ebenezer's reappearance, forgetting all about this item of news, which really did not interest him, since he had no South African connections.

The dinner was a good but frugal one, and mainly Mr Ebenezer Jackson made the conversation. He talked about South Africa, about Australia, about the fortunes that could he made by young men of enterprise willing to take a very slight risk, and about the foolishness of spending large sums of money on gilt-edged securities which do not yield an adequate return.

"By the way, Dobbly, I have an investment which would interest a young man like you. Unfortunately, I am too old to see the thing through."

"Indeed, sir, answered Dob, interested.

"There is a coal mine (not a gold mine) in South Africa in which I hold a very large number of shares. I bought, intending to exploit the property. I might say that there is little or no coal on the property, but I am perfectly sure that underneath the coal you will find gold. And that, property," he added impressively, "may be worth anything up to a million."

"Or down to tuppence," suggested Dob flippantly.

That was the annoying thing about Dob. When you thought you had him thoroughly impressed, he would turn the conversation with an unexpected piece of facetiousness.

Mr Jackson was, however, a man of considerable experience. He knew when to check, and when to make play. He smiled at Dob's observation as though it were the best joke in the world, and tactfully changed the conversation.

They had arrived at the coffee stage of dinner when Mr Jackson's elderly servant came in.

"Miss Mona is on the telephone, sir. She said it is very important."

"Indeed!" exclaimed Ebenezer, with well-feigned surprise. "Miss Jackson knows that I can't use the telephone just now owing to my earache."

Ho looked at Dobbly.

"My dear fellow, will you be good enough to go to the 'phone for me and take whatever message my niece has?"

"With all the pleasure in life," replied Dob, for a moment deceived. He hurried out into the hall where the instrument was kept.

"Is that you, Uncle Eb?" asked Miss Jackson's voice.

"No, it is Dobbly. Mr Jackson asked me to answer the telephone."

There was a pause.

"Well, this is rather important," went on the sweet tones of Miss Mona, "but I am sure I can trust you, Mr Dobbly. Will you tell uncle that I have received a cablegram from South Africa saying that a large deposit of coal has been found on the Ecfontein property?"

"Certainly, Miss Jackson," responded Dob solemnly. "When was the message received? Shall I tell him that?"

"Only half-an-hour ago. It was despatched from Johannesburg this morning."

"Thank you." Dob hung up the telephone receiver.

Half the success of the confidence trickster depends upon the simplicity of his plans; the other half on the stupidity of his victim.

Mr Jackson's plan was simple; indeed it was childish. Dob was a willing victim. He returned to his host with a fine air of carelessness.

"Miss Jackson wanted to tell you that she has had a cablegram from South Africa, saying that gold has been found on some property or other—I didn't quite catch the name."

Ebenezer smiled within himself; he knew very well that Dob had heard the name, and that "coal" and not "gold" was the word he heard.

He waited for the development of his scheme. It came just before Dob took his departure.

"By the way, Mr Jackson," he spoke with that same indifference, "what were those shares you were talking about?"

"Ecfontein Collieries?" asked Ebenezer.

"Yes, that was it; what do you want for them? They are not worth very much in the market, are they?"

"Well you can have them for a shilling a share," said Ebenezer, "and in making this offer to you I am, of course, giving you an opportunity which very few young men are offered."

Dob seemed to be considering.

"I'll tell you what, Mr Jackson—by the way, how many have you for disposal?"

"A hundred thousand," answered Ebenezer, and Dob nodded.

"What I will do is this—I will buy a twenty-four hours' option on the hundred thousand, and will pay you one hundred pounds cash for the privilege."

"What you want," interrupted Ebenezer, a little annoyed, "is the option of buying a hundred thousand shares at a shilling. Well, Mr Dobbly, I don't know that that is good business from my point of view, and it is customary for an option buyer to pay something for the privilege."

"As I say, I'll pay you a hundred pounds," repeated Dob promptly, and Mr Ebenezer Jackson agreed with almost indecent haste.

Dob went up to the club a very thoughtful young man. There he found a stockbroker who was by way of being a friend of his.

"Do you know anything about Ecfontein Collieries?"

Mr Mansar, to whom the question was addressed, turned a smiling face upon him.

"Do I know anything of them? I know there is a piece of waste ground in the world that bears that title."

"What are the shares worth?"

"The price of wastepaper, which is very little just now. Why?"

"Because I've bought an option on a hundred thousand."

"Goad lord!" gasped Mansar. "You've been dining with old Ebenezer."

Dob nodded.

"Whatever induced you to take this rash step?" demanded Mansar, in surprise. "My dear fellow, the shares aren't worth that"—he snapped his fingers. "The old boy has been trying to get rid of them for years. When I tell yon that ten thousand of the Ecfontein Colliery shares aren't worth a Denikin rouble*, you'll understand."

[* An allusion to the currency issued by White Army leader Anton Ivanovich Denikin during the civil war following the Russian Revolution.]

"Those shares are worth from half-a-crown to three shillings each," interrupted Dob calmly. "They may even be worth five shillings. And what is more, old Ebenezer, who invited me to dinner to-night with the object of skinning me, is going to pay that price per share, or my name is not Archibald Dobbly."

The news went through Brackton like wildfire. It began at the golf club, and radiated through every home in a village which was notorious for its intelligent services.

Dob bad been stung.

Nobody quite knew why Dob the Dud was so called, or why he had been christened with that unflattering title. Perhaps it was his monocle and his general vacant expression; certainly nobody ever remembered his having committed so dudish an act before.

The principal topic of conversation on the way to the city the next morning was the skinning of Dob. Mr Ebenezer Jackson did not share in the gossip, for he went to town by car. Of one thing only he was certain—he had made a hundred pounds out of Dob, and he did not doubt that the moment Dob got into touch with a sane stockbroker the bargain would be repudiated.

Dob himself had to bear a great deal of good-natured chaff.

"I understand you've got an office in town where you give advice to people," said one of his neighbours. "If I were you, Dob, I'd go straight to that office and find somebody who is competent to whisper in your ear—'Don't buy Ecfontein.'"

Dob smiled genially.

"What you want," suggested another, "is not so much a friend as a nurse. There isn't one of us that Ebenezer hasn't tried to sell those infernal shares to."

"I'll bet you a hundred that I sell them back to Ebenezer at a profit?"

Mr Verity, the banker, to whom he had made the offer, shook his hand.

"I do not ordinarily bet," he replied, "but I bet you twenty pounds that you're stung for a hundred."

"I'll take you," answered Dob promptly, "and if you think that this is the first time Ebenezer has tried to work his shares off on me, you're mistaken. He doesn't remember the fact, but the very first day I was introduced to him, he started talking Ecfontein Collieries."

"He's a mean old devil," said Verity, "and I wish yon luck."

"There's one thing I'd like to ask you, Mr Verily, and probably you'll be able to give me the information I want. Can you recall anybody who has ever got the best of Ebenezer?"

Mr Verity considered.

"Yes—Franks & Franks; they are Ebenezer's 'bête noire.' They have bested him in two or three deals, and he can hardly speak their name without growing apoplectic."

"Franks & Franks," repeated Dob slowly, "I think I know one of the partners. Thank you, Mr Verity."

He went to his office, and after examining the correspondence, made his way to the palatial offices of Franks & Franks, in Threadneedle Street.

The junior partner, Mr Harry Franks, a pleasant Hebrew, welcomed Dob with open arms. They had met in France, when this bald-headed, middle-aged man, was the driver of a Red Cross ambulance.

"Do you know anything about Ecfontein Collieries, Franks?" asked Dob.

The other looked at him soberly, and handed him a cigar.

"Don't tell me that they've landed you with a parcel."

"I've an option on a hundred thousand," explained Dob, "and I paid a hundred pounds for the privilege."

"Stop the cheque and plead temporary derangement," advised Mr Franks promptly. "Ecfonteins! My dear chap, they are not worth the paper they're printed on."

He looked at Dob with a startled expression.

"Don't say Ebenezer Jackson has caught you?"

There was a twinkle in Dob's eye.

"I bought an option—as a matter of fact, the cheque isn't paid, but it will be, of course. I've agreed to give that sum for the privilege of purchasing the shares. What is more," he added slowly, "I am going to take up my option."

Mr Franks jumped out of his chair.

"You're mad," he exclaimed.

"At least," continued Dob, with a laugh, "I'm going to take it up if you'll let me write a letter on your notepaper. I'll strike out your address and name. You see, Franks, I'm getting rather tired of being regarded as a dud. There are moments when it doesn't worry me, but there are times when it irritates me beyond expression. Ebenezer has challenged my intelligence so definitely that I could not but take the challenge up. It is not sufficient that I should reject his preposterous offer. I must hit back at him. Now, if you will let me write on your paper a letter accepting his offer, taking up the option, I think you will have some fun."

Mr Franks looked dubious.

"All right," he eventually complied. "It's your funeral. Sit down at my desk and write your letter, but you're losing money, and I hate to see a young fellow throwing it away. If yon want an investment, buy Madeira Banana Lands. I've just had a wireless from Madeira—"

But Dob sat at the big ornate desk, took a sheet of notepaper from the rack and, running his pen through the firm's address, wrote in a hurried scrawl:—

"Dear Mr Jackson—

"This is to notify you that I am taking up the option of the whole hundred thousand. Arrange for the immediate transfer of these shares and I will call at your office this afternoon at two o'clock with the necessary cheque. Under no circumstances allow your Ecfontein Colliery shares to pass into any possession but mine.—Yours in haste,

"Archibald Dobbly."

"Read that." he said, handing the letter to his friend.

Mr Franks read it and his condition of mind, when he had finished reading it, made his protest almost incoherent.

"You're—you're stark, staring mad," he gasped. "There is neither gold, coal, nor iron on that property. You are simply throwing your money into the gutter."

"We shall see," answered Dob, smiling.

He despatched the letter by special messenger and went back to his office. He hardly reached there when the telephone bell rang. It was Mr Jackson's voice at the other end of the wire.

"Is that you, Dobbly?"

"Yes."

"You're taking those shares?"

"Rather." Dob put as much exultation as he could get into his voice.

"I see you wrote from Franks & Franks," went on Ebenezer.

"Yes," said Dob. "I—er—know Mr Franks."

"Did he advise you to buy them?"

There was a silence. At last Dob replied—

"I'd rather you didn't ask that question. Mr Jackson. Mr Franks is a very old friend of mine, and I don't feel that it is fair to him that I should reveal any of our conversation of this morning."

"Will you come round to the office at once?" pleaded Ebenezer, after a pause, and his voice was shaky.

"Will you have the transfer ready?" asked Dob, winking at the ceiling.

"Come along round," was the diplomatic reply. "Take a cab—or—I'll pay for it." Jackson had a suite of offices in Queen Victoria Street, and Dob was there in ten minutes. He found the jobber pacing his room like a caged lion.

"Good morning," cried Dob cheerfully, planking the cheque upon the table. "I've brought round the five thousand, Mr Jackson, and have made it payable to bearer, so that you can send your clerk round and cash the cheque immediately."

"Well, the fact is, Dobbly, I thought that I'd better wait before I transferred these shares. You see, I've been trying to get into communication with South Africa. Anything may have happened there, and I find that the cable has not been working."

"Oh, it must have been working," said Dob cheerfully. "Your niece had a cablegram from Johannesburg only yesterday."

Mr Ebenezer Jackson looked uncomfortable.

"That must have been despatched some time ago, and delayed. No, Dobbly, if you don't mind we will just wait until I get an answer to the cable I've sent to my Johannesburg agent."

Dob shook his head.

"That I can't allow," he responded quietly. "You have sold me an option on the shares, and I am taking up that option.

"It is an opportunity, as you said last night, which no young man can afford to lose."

"Has Franks heard anything from South Africa?" asked the other suspiciously, and Dob was silent.

"He has, has he?" Mr Jackson dropped his hand with geniality on Dob's shoulder.

"Now, now, my boy," he continued waggishly, "let me know what Franks has discovered."

"I think Mr Franks said that he had had a wireless message from Madeira," answered Dob reluctantly, "but I am not in—er—a position to tell you its contents. That is entirely Mr Franks' business, and unless he gave me permission I certainly could not abuse his confidence. Anyway, that doesn't matter, does it?" he smiled. "You have sold me the option, and there is nothing else for me to do but to take the transfer."

Mr Jackson's agitation was almost tragic.

"I tell you what, Dobbly. I am going to make a confession to you that I wouldn't make to anybody else. Those shares were given me by my Uncle George, a man for whom I have the utmost veneration. Ever since I sold you the option I have been conscience-stricken. I have sold shares which my Uncle George asked me, almost with his dying breath, to keep in the family. Now, what do you say? Suppose we make a little bargain? I'll return you your hundred pounds and give you, say, another hundred on top, if you tear up the option I gave you."

"That, I couldn't agree to sir," he replied. "I'm pretty certain that I ran get five shillings a share for Ecfontein Collieries."

"Five shillings a share!" screamed Jackson. "Rubbish! Who will give you five shillings a share unless—" he frowned heavily. "Now tell me, Dobbly, what have you learnt about this stock?"

"I only know, sir," began Dob, and stopped. "Perhaps I had better not tell you. There is my cheque, and I want the shares."

"Now, don't be precipitate, my boy," cautioned Mr Jackson, beads of perspiration standing on hi pallid brow. "If they are worth five shillings to other people, they are worth five shillings to me. Now, suppose I take the whole of your stock over at, let us say, three shillings a share?"

After haggling and bargaining for nearly half on hour Dob went out with a cheque for £15,000 from Jackson in his pocket.

Mr Jackson waited until the door closed on Dob, then seized the telephone with feverish hands and called up Franks & Franks. There were times when he could not forbear to gloat over his enemies.

"Is that you, Franks? I've bought those shares from Dobbly—the Ecfontein Collieries."

"You've bought them?" was the incredulous reply. "Do you mean to say that you've bought them back from him?"

"I do," cried Ebenezer, triumphantly.

"Then you're a bigger fool than I thought you were. Dob said he would stick you with them, and you've cost me two hundred. I bet him two hundred he wouldn't. What did you pay for them?"

"Three shillings a share," wailed Mr Ebenezer Jackson, and there came a groan from the other end of the 'phone.

"He's won! What an infernal dud."

"I don't know that he is so much of a dud," quavered Ebenezer. "I've just given him an open cheque for fifteen thousand."

"I wasn't referring to Dob. I was referring to you," was the cruel reply.

CHAPTER V

THE HAUNTED HOUSE

In the days when Brackton was "country," and the town con-sisted of a village inn, a church, a parsonage, and a few scattered cottages, there came to this old-world spot an eccentric banker named Durand. His eccentricity was manifested by the erection of a great Georgian house, and the purchase of a great deal of land in the neighbourhood.

Brackton was off the stage coach route. There was no hunting and little shooting, and the friends of Josiah Durand regarded his purchase as the first sign of a weakening intellect.

After a lapse of a hundred years Brackton came into its own and developed from village to town. Right opposite the stern old Georgian house William Durand, the son of Josiah, erected the first bank that Brackton had known, a branch of his own private bank in London.

It is not necessary to give the history of Durand's Bank, or its subsequent amalgamation with the London, Eastern and Welsh Banking Corporation Ltd. John Durand, the present holder of the title, had long since given up the ramshackle house about which had grown a wilderness of modern villas, and was living on a little estate which he had laid out on Brackton Hill.

But Durand's Bank was still a power, for although its amalgamation was an accomplished fact, the old name stuck. But the ancient house erected by the first of the Durands stood empty and desolate, and became a frequent subject of discussion at the club.

"I wonder you don't give it to Dob, sir. It would make a fine local office for him," suggested Mr Jacques Richter.

Mr Richter was one of the fashionable young men of Brackton, and was, moreover, the prospective son-in-law of John Durand. He traced his parentage back to a family of Alsatians and indignantly repudiated the suggestion that there was a drop of German blood in his veins, pointing triumphantly to his service during the war. Nobody quite knew what those services were, but he had certainly worn a uniform, in which he had appeared at too frequent intervals in Brackton.

John Durand laughed.

"I shall pull the old place down one of these days," he said, "though I shall hate losing it."

"You'll have the County Council on your back if you don't," warned the Borough Surveyor who was one of the audience. "If you delay long in pulling it down, it will fall down."

"Not it," answered Durand emphatically. "The builders of Georgian days built for eternity. Still, it is a sin and shame that the house should remain vacant, with the land unoccupied. I'll think it over."

John Durand was always "thinking it over." He never got any further, apparently.

Mr Richter walked home with him that night and Mr Archibald Dobbly came again into the conversation.

"He's a queer fellow, is Dob," remarked John Durand, "but I like him. He is in some curious business, isn't he?"

"He's a 'professional friend and confidential adviser,'" replied Richter solemnly, and then chuckled. "Why don't you go to Dob and ask him what he would do with the house?"

"I won't go as far as that," smiled Durand.

"Why don't you consult May?" asked Richter maliciously. John winced, for this [flighty?] daughter was the real master of his household and ruled him with a rod of iron. An only daughter, she had been spoilt by her [doting?] father, and he was now reaping what he had sown.

"I never bother May with things like that," he said shortly.

They found the young lady in question in the drawing room. She was reading the [latest?] novel, and Mr Durand made a face when he saw its title.

"I wish you wouldn't read that kind of book, May."

"Why not?" she inquired coolly. "Really, daddy, you are silly. The modern young woman is not half so squeamish as her grandmother and I rather like this story."

John Durand said nothing. He had learnt from experience that to commence an argument with his daughter meant that he would be very badly worsted. Consequently, he was glad to switch the conversation to Dob, at the mention of whom Mary put down her book and listened with interest.

"I can't quite make him out, dad," she interrupted. "He seems such an awful ass, and yet he has the most charming manners."

"Most awful asses have," interrupted Mr Jacques Richter good-humouredly. "I'm afraid old Dob will always be a dud."

"From what I have heard," cut in Mr John Durand drily, "he is not half the dud you imagine him to be."

"I was suggesting to your father that he could consult Dob," Richter went on. "You know he has an office in the City, and gives advice for a fee. He is a sort of professional friend—I think that's what he calls 'Professional Friend.'"

Her eyebrows went up and her lips parted in a smile. "What a grand idea! Oh, daddy, do think of something."

"Something?" asked the puzzled Mr Durand.

"Can't we consult him about something? The house. What an excellent idea. You know, I've always told you that you ought to pull it down and build a block of workmen's flats. The working-class quarter of Brackton is shockingly overcrowded."

"I don't intend asking Dob's advice on what I shall do with my property," smiled Mr Durand good-humouredly. "I'm going to the smoking-room. If you think of any brilliant idea, let me know."

"I've got it," cried the girl when her father had left. "Oh, it's such a splendid idea, Jacques."

He looked at her languishingly.

"If it is your idea—"

"Oh, stop," she scoffed. "Don't be silly, Jacques."

Her attitude towards her fiance was one of bored tolerance. There were moments when Mr Jacques Richter wished that the marriage knot had been tied, so that he could express his sentiments without taking the risk of losing what promised to be a profitable investment.

"We'll haunt the house," she exclaimed excitedly.

"Haunt it?"

"You know, we'll haunt it with mysterious bells and clanking chains and strange, weird shapes that move through the darkness—"

"Whatever are you talking about?" he asked, bewildered.

"I mean that we're going to haunt Durand House," she repeated impatiently. "We're going to employ Dob to lay the ghost, and we'll scare the life out of him."

She threw back her head and her peal of laughter reached Mr Durand in his study.

He smiled in sympathy, but he was loss amused when the idea was put to him.

"It's hardly fair on Dobbly." he objected. "Really. I don't think I can let you do it."

"You're not only going to let me do it, daddy, you're going to help. I need a nice middle-aged ghost like you."

Mr Durand groaned, yet he was not so old that he could not appreciate a good joke. Protesting a little feebly that it was not fair, he nevertheless entered into the conspiracy.

Dob was very surprised the next mooring, when a pretty and demure figure walked into his office smiling at his embarrassment. He knew the girl, had admired her secretly, and was invariably embarrassed in her presence, which was not like Dob.

He got up, very red of face, and brought a chair forward.

"This is very unexpected, Miss Durand."

Only for a moment did the girl's resolution waver. With her keen feminine instinct she sensed his feelings for her, and was momentarily repentant; but her penitence did not last very long.

"I have come on a very important, mysterious errand, Mr Dobbly," she began, solemnly. "It's about Durand House."

"Durand House?" he repeated. "Oh, that old Georgian house in High Street? A place with a wilderness of a garden. It belongs to your people, doesn't it?"

"It's been in the family for hundreds of years," she told him.

She was rather vague as to the exact length of time, but she was not far out. "And, Mr Dobbly," she continued, "Durand House in haunted."

"Haunted?" He regarded her inquiringly.

"Haunted," she repeated emphatically.

"This is news to me," observed Dob. "I have lived in Brackton for quite a time, but I've never heard of that before."

"I discovered it," the girl went on, "quite by accident."

"Does your father know?"

She nodded.

"It was he who suggested that I should come to see you."

Dob smiled.

"What am I to do? Lay the ghost?"

She drew her chair nearer.

"Mr Dobbly," she lowered her voice, "these manifestations appear every Thursday night between ten and twelve o'clock. A friend of mine has been watching the home, and he has seen strange, ghostly lights moving inside. He has heard the clanking of chains, and wild, eerie shrieks."

"You want me to go to the haunted house to discover what's the cause, eh?" he smiled.

May inclined her head.

"Have you seen these lights yourself?"

Only for a second she hesitated.

"Yes, I saw them last week," she proceeded glibly. "Our bank is on the opposite side of the road, and I watched the place from the cashier's room a upstairs."

"Well, that's rum," mused Dob, rubbing his chin. "Of course, I'll undertake the job with pleasure. Have you got a key? How do I get in?"

She opened her bag and took out a large key, the type that ancient householders carried at their belt, with a plug of wood in the hole to keep out the dust.

"It's a curious commission." He spoke with a half smile, and she thought he looked wonderfully boyish. "But I'll be most happy to do it for you, Miss Durand," he concluded, raising his eyes to hers, and again she felt a little prick of conscience.

She burst into her father's study that evening.

"He's going to do it, daddy. Now, where is Jacques? He promised to be here to fix everything up."

"What do you propose doing?"

"We'll get into the house at nine o'clock," she said, speaking rapidly. "We shall just have time to fix up a few contraptions."

"Such as?" asked her father.

"Oh, phosphorous paint, flashes of green fire, and clanking chains. We'll do the groaning ourselves."

"You don't expect me to go down there and play the fool, do you?"

"I want you to come, daddy. I really can't be in an empty house with Jacques Richter without a chaperone."

Mr Durand groaned.

"Yes, that groan will do admirably for to-night. You'll have to do the groaning, daddy."

Her father grinned.

"There's no fool like an old fool," he laughed, "but I suppose I'll have to humour you."

The question of chaperoning the girl and Mr Richter did not arise. Mr Richter put in a reluctant appearance a few minutes later, complaining that he had twisted his ankle and couldn't possibly accompany the party.

"You're shamming," she scoffed. "I believe you're scared.

"Nonsense," replied Jacques Richter loudly. "What do you mean by 'scared?' Didn't I serve in the war, and would anybody who served in the war—?"

"You served in an Army Service Corps Depot at Plymouth," she said quickly. "You were even beyond the reach of Zeppelins!"

Richter muttered something under his breath. But on one point he was adamant: he could not and would not go to the haunted house, and Mr Durand and May went alone, the former growing more and more uncomfortable as they approached the house.

Archibald Dobbly was puzzled. He did not believe in ghosts, nor could he conceive that a sensible, pretty girl like May Durand could have any foolish notions on the subject. Still, she was a woman, and to him, one of the very few women in the world who counted, and she must be humoured.

He went up into his bedroom, took a revolver from a cupboard, looked at it for some time and then, remembering that the house my possibly be occupied by some person who had no right to be there, he slipped it into his pocket, along with an electric torch, after replacing the battery with a new one. Then, taking his bicycle from the shed behind the house, he cycled gently into the town.

It was nearly ten o'clock when he passed through the iron gates of Durand House. He put his bicycle against a tree, extinguishing the light lest it should attract the attention of a passing policeman.

He pulled on a pair of felt over-slippers, which he had purchased that day for the purpose. They fitted over his boots, and enabled him to move noiselessly.

He walked up the flagged path, mounted the stairs, tried the key in the lock, and it turned readily. He entered the house and, closing the door softly behind him, flashed a beam of light along the passage. Halfway up the passage was an old mat. The house was apparently devoid of furniture, and dust lay on the floor.

He had lifted his foot to take a step, when he heard a curious sound. It was rumble and thud at such regular intervals as to suggest that some machine was working in the basement of the house. He stepped eagerly forward, switched off his light, and reached the mat. He put one foot on it, when a blood-curdling yell made him spring back. For a moment his hair stood on end, and then he laughed softly to himself.

"A claxon horn," he muttered.

Lifting the mat, he found a little bell-push, a knob extending upwards, and a thin strand of wire running to the stair.

Then for the first time he realised that he was being made the victim of a practical joke. But that realisation gave way immediately to another. The thud and rumble had suddenly ceased.

There was a door leading to what was apparently the front drawing-room. He opened this gingerly and went in, sending the beams of his torch into each corner. It was empty, and the ceiling hung with cobwebs. It communicated with a back drawing-room by a pair of folding doors. These he opened and stopped astonished for the floor was piled with earth that reached half way to the ceiling. And then he heard a sound. It was only the slightest shuffle of a foot on the stone stairs, but there was something about that stealthy movement which set his nerves on edge. He slipped his pistol from his pocket, drew back the steel jacket, and thumbed-up the safety catch.

He listened at the door. The house had been solidly built and no floor-board creaked as he moved.

There was no light in the passage, which narrowed as it met the stairs, but he wee conscious that somebody was there in the dark. He drew himself back flat against the wall of the drawing-room. Presently he was rewarded by seeing a beam of light in the corridor, and a low voice whispered—

"It was a car outside."

There were two people, and he wondered who they were. The voices were not those of people who might be employed to carry out a practical joke and, anyway, they would not have been surprised at the yell of the claxon.

After waiting for some time, Dob moved cautiously from his place of concealment and continued his journey along the passage. Twice he flashed his lamp and saw a doorway under the stairs. Evidently it was from mere that the men had come. He was moving towards the door when he saw a crumpled piece of paper near his feet and, stooping, picked it up. He had seen May Durand's writing before, and he recognised it immediately. It was a little list written on a slip of paper, and by the light of his electric torch he read—

"Claxon horn in passage, figures on first floor landing, chains in room upstairs, daddy to wear white nightgown."

Hearing a sound, he flicked out the torch light. It was the resumption of the thud and rumble he had heard when he entered the house. What did it mean? It was clear to him now that the girl had contemplated a practical joke on him, and for a moment he felt a little sore, but where was she? Obviously her father was to be in the house and she must have been there too, to have left that piece of paper. What was the meaning of all the earth in the room?

He opened the little door under the stair and listened. Faintly came the sound of whispering voices as he stared down into the darkness. The steps led to a basement apartment, the old kitchen of the house, he guessed. He went down noiselessly, step by step, putting one hand on the wall and feeling gingerly with his foot until he came to the passage below.

There was no sign of light, but the low murmur of voices still came to him. He crept along the passage, and by a momentary flash of his lamp saw a door, from behind which the sound came. Again he heard the rumble, and at once its meaning dawned on him. It was the sound of a wheel-barrow running along a plunk, and the thuds were caused by the wheels bumping against the space where wood met wood.

Reaching the door, he tried the handle cautiously. It opened, and showed a thin slither of light. The room into which he stepped was unoccupied—it was the old scullery—and from thence led through a doorless opening to the vast underground kitchen of Durand House.

Now the voices were clear.

"If you made him give you the keys, it would save us a lot of trouble," suggested one.

"The keys, you fool?" snorted the other. "We'd look fine opening the doors of the bank at this hour of the night, shouldn't we? No, we'll be into the strong room by two o'clock. Laurie is working the light on the steel lining now."

There was a pause.

"What are you going to do with these two?" asked the first voice.

Dob's heart leapt.

"They can stay down here until they're found," replied the other, "but it wouldn't be a bad idea," he added, "if we took the girl with us. That would make them careful about coming after us."

There was another long pause, broken only by the noise made by the wheel barrow. Then a third voice spoke.

"That's your last load; now we've got plenty of room to work. Thank God we shan't have to take the stuff upstairs to-morrow. It nearly broke my back. Laurie's going to take the girl," he added.

"I thought he would," remarked the first voice.

"You'll not take me with you." It was May's clear voice that spoke.

"You shut up," ordered the first man, gruffly. "If you don't go with us quietly, we'll settle your old man. This would mean a lifer for all of us, and I'd just as soon be hung."

"You blackguards, you'll pay for this." Now it was John Durand speaking.

Dob, creeping along the wall, glimpsed through the open apace in the direction of the voice. Durand, his wrists tied together, was fastened to a chair by a broad strap which was passed round his waist. His ankles were corded to the legs of the chair. The girl was free, and was sitting right up, uncowed by the danger.

Then it was that Dob stepped from his place of concealment. He took in the scene at one glance. The low kitchen, the two paraffin lamps burning on the table, the three men, one leaning on the handle of his barrow and stripped almost to his waist, the other two, their clothes soiled with the earth they had been removing.

He met the girl's eyes for a moment, and she smiled.

At that smile the three men swung round to see whet she was looking at.

"Keep still!" Dob ordered, handling his pistol carelessly, "and don't shout."

The biggest of the men, a fellow with a short stubby beard, spoke first.

"Who are you!" he demanded.

"I am a layer of ghosts," answered Dob, and then, not turning his head, "unfasten your father, Miss Durand."

He took a clasp knife from his pocket, and threw it towards her. A few minutes later John Durand was standing by his side.

"I think, Mr Durand, you had better take your daughter out, and bring a couple of the constabulary," smiled Dob. "Please be careful not to step on the mat."

The girl flushed, and dropped her eyes before his.

"I am sorry," she said in a low voice.

"And I am jolly glad," replied Dob, cheerfully.

He heard them stumbling on the stairs. He heard the street door open, and with a prayer of thankfulness in his heart he realised the girl was safe.

"Now, gentlemen," he began, and then, from the darkness of a gap in the wall at the further end of the kitchen came a bright pencil of flame. The bullet just missed Dob's cheek, and crashed into the wall behind him. Then he leapt to cover.

Again the unseen shooter fired, the bullet carrying away the toe-cap of Dob's boot and a generous portion of felt slipper. Keeping close to the edge of the wall, he fired twice in the direction of the hole, and the place was plunged into darkness.

"Rush him!" boomed a voice, but Dob was through the door and up the stairs in half a dozen seconds. He stopped at the top of the stairs and looked down.

"You can only come up one at a time," he said, "and you'll go down one at a time."

They did not attempt to repeat the rushing tactics and, when half a dozen policemen arrived, they found a fairly tractable gang to arrest.

A careful search of the kitchen revealed the fact that these men had bored a tunnel under the bank, and had reached the steel walls of the strong room, which they were cutting when the unexpected arrival of John Durand and his daughter had created a diversion.

The terrified girl and her father had been seized and taken into the basement.

"They must have been working for a month," explained John Durand, puffing at his cigar that night, before going to bed. "Of course, they knew nobody ever visited the house, and it was a fairly easy job for them to break in and establish their head-quarters. They stole their planks and barrows from Jay's, the builder, by the way."

But Miss May Durand was not worrying about the methods the burglars employed. She was sitting on the hearth-rug before the fire, clasping her knees and staring into the flames.

"It's rather a good job Jacques could not come to-night," remarked John Durand, "and it really wasn't a bad idea of yours, May, to employ Dob the Dud."

She looked up at her father coldly.

"I think Dob the Dud is a very vulgar nickname," she answered severely, "and I'm awfully glad that Jacques wasn't there."

CHAPTER VI

THE PEAR-SHAPED DIAMOND

Mr Archibald Dobbly found it difficult to fix the day and hour when he began to regard Jacques Richter in the light of a rival. Dob told himself a dozen times a day that he had no title whatever to May Durand's affection. It is true he had rendered her a very great service, but that debt had been cancelled when her father had sent him a cheque, which, although he was loath to receive, he could find no excuse for refusing.

Jacques Richter was of Alsatian origin, a fact that he never ceased to impress upon all and sundry. It mattered little to Dob whether he was Alsatian or darnation. Dob's principal grievance was that he existed at all. It may be said that Jacques, Richter resented Dob's appearance in company with the girl as strenuously.

Jacques was an elegant young man of twenty-eight, who always gave the impression that he had stepped from the bands of a small army of valets. He was engaged by day in some light occupation, which did not in any way disarrange the set of his cravat or dim the lustre of his patent shoes. There were many who thought that his main occupation was the hunting of John Durand's heiress.

Dob in his turn did not take so uncharitable a view. He regarded Richter as a man of some means, and when his engagement to May Durand was announced, Dob took it for granted that her father had made the necessary inquiries into the young man's financial position. He did not realise then how dominant a personality was this high-spirited daughter of the banker, or the extent of her autocracy. It had never occurred to John Durand to oppose her slightest wish, and he had accepted Jacques Richter as he had accepted every other choice of his daughter, in the faith that she would come out on top.

It was a few days after the adventure in the alleged haunted house that Dob first saw the outward and visible signs of May Durand's engagement. It was a diamond ring of an extraordinary character. The stone was so large that upon any other hand than hers it would have appeared vulgar. It ran almost the length of the girl's finger joint, and when he saw it he gasped, He was taking tea with May Durand, and it was his good fortune that neither Mr Richter nor her father had put in an appearance.

"Yes, it is a beautiful ring. Jacques gave it to me a month ago."

"It is a beauty," agreed Dob.

"Jacques brought it from Paris," she told him calmly. "He paid a hundred thousand francs for it."

Dob smiled inwardly. It was so like May to insist on knowing the price. Or had Jacques carelessly volunteered the information?

"He is a very fortunate man," observed Dob, and she looked at him queerly.

"Do you think so! I don't think you would say that if you knew the immense responsibility which he has undertaken."

Dob coughed.

"When is this undertaking to begin?"

"When am I going to be married?" asked the practical May. "Oh, in a year, possibly sooner," and then the conversation drifted to other topics.

John Durand came in, and later Mr Richter, looking more than ever like a fashion plate. He shot a glance, which was not one of kindly welcome, at Dob, and greeted his fiancée with a certain affected ostentation.

It was during the conversation which followed that Dob learnt for the first time that the girl had met her future husband whilst travelling on the Continent.

From the vague reference Richter made to his "home," Dob gathered that he had a château on the Loire, and a family interest in other estates in France. What amazed him was the extraordinary frankness of the girl, and the absence of any mystery about their relationship.

"Mr Dobbly has been asking when I am going to married, Jacques."

"And what did you tell him?' he asked eagerly.

"I told him that it would be in a year or so," she answered, with a curious little smile, and Jacques' face fell.

"But," he stammered, "you told me—next month."

"I have changed my mind," May informed him calmly.

Was Dob's fancy playing him a trick, or did the imperturbable face of Mr Jacques Richter go a shade paler?

"But I've mode all my arrangements for next month," he protested.

"And I have made all my arrangements for next year. Now, Jacques, don't let us argue on this indelicate subject before Mr Dobbly, who is young and impressionable."

Dob made his adieux soon after, and was glad to get away from an atmosphere which was rapidly becoming strained.

He saw Mr Richter the next morning on the train, and Jacques cut him dead. Dob was astounded more than hurt; amused rather than annoyed. When he left the railway terminus he thought he had seen the last of Jacques for the day, but in this he was mistaken. He had occasion to lunch at a big restaurant in the West End, his guest being a new client who wanted advice about some rubber shares. Dob, with the assistance of a friend, was launching forth in the direction of a financial expert.

They were half way through the meal when, glancing up, he saw on the other side of the room, two men sitting at a table, and the back of one of these was familiar to him. He could not very well mistake the perfectly cut coat, the beautifully pomaded hair, of Mr Richter. His companion was an elderly man with a grey beard and, by his gesticulations, was evidently a foreigner. He was apparently very angry, and there was a despondent curve to Mr Richter's back which rather fascinated Dob.

He observed them idly and then, turning his attention again to his client, he let the matter pass from his mind.

When his luncheon was finished the waiter came, and he paid his bill. On leaving he interrogated the head waiter.

"Who is that old gentleman over there, the fellow with the beard? A foreigner isn't he."

The head waiter glanced at the pair Dob had indicated.

"Oh, no," he replied, "he has a shop in town," and be told Dob the name.

Dob thanked him, and again the incident closed in his mind.

That evening he met May Durand on the golf course and played a round with her.

"You don't like Jacques, do you!" she eked unexpectedly.

"I don't dislike him," answered the cautious Dob, "even though he cut me dead this morning."

She laughed.

"Did he really?" she exclaimed, her eyes dancing with merriment. "How very funny!"

"It was a bit funny," admitted Dob. "I don't know what I've done to your young man."

"Don't you?" she inquired demurely.

A second later she swung at a ball and sent it flying. When they resumed their trudge she talked about something altogether different, and the name of Jacques' Richter did not arise until they were walking home from the club.

"Do you still run that absurd little office of yours?"

"I run an absurdly little office," corrected Dob with a smile.

"I mean are you still a professional friend and adviser?"

"I am indeed," said Dob. "If you want any advice out of business hours, you can have it for a little extra fee."

She looked at him again with that strange, mocking light in her eyes.

"I've a jolly good mind to ask you for advice. Suppose I came to you and asked you whether I ought to marry Jacques Richter, what would you say?"

Dob went red, then while.

"That is an unfair question," he replied quietly, "and I have an idea nobody knows how unfair it is better than you."

She was silent after that, and when he parted from her he said penitently—

"I've been rather a bore, haven't I?"

She shook her head.

"I've been rather a fool, that's all," she remarked, offering her hand.

She was not at the club the next day, nor the next. On the third day Dob was closing his office, pulling down the top of his desk, when there was a timid knock at the door.

"Come in!" he cried.

He recognised the girl who came in. She was a servant at the Durand's house, and his heart came up into his throat. Had May sent for him, he wondered? Then, something about the demeanour of the girl attracted him. Her eyes were red and her face discoloured with weeping, and when she spoke her voice was shaking.

"I hope you don't mind my coming to you Mr Dobbly," she began, "but I heard Mr Durand speak about you, and I'm so upset that I don't know what to do. I have nobody I can consult."

She was distressed, and every sentence had a sob in it.

"Now, please calm yourself, miss—I don't know your name."

"I am Alice, sir—Alice Girton."

"Well, Alice, you must not be upset. What has happened? There is nothing wrong with Miss Durand, is there?" he demanded quickly, with a sudden tightening of his heart.

"No, sir, there's nothing wrong with Miss Durand. I thought you would have heard—oh, it's dreadful, and Mr Richter has been so terribly cruel to me." At this she broke down, and it was some time before she could control her voice.

"You have got to tell me what has happened," Dob spoke kindly, "and try to think that you are talking not about yourself, but about somebody else. I can't help you unless I know."

"It's about Miss Durand's ring," sobbed the girl.

"Do you mean her engagement ring?" inquired Dob sharply.

The girl nodded.

"The big diamond one?"

She nodded again.

"Mr Durand wanted to send for you last night," she gulped, "but Mr Richter wouldn't hear of it. He said awful things about you. He called you, Dob the Dud—"

"Never mind what he called me," smiled Dob, fixing his monocle, and showing his white teeth in a grin. "I quite expect Mr Richter would say some very unpleasant things if he had the slightest provocation. Is the ring lost?"

She told him it was, and gradually the whole story came out.

"Mr Richter called last night, and I think he and Miss Durand had a little tiff, but they were all right at dinner. Miss May was wearing her ring. I saw it as I was serving the soup. Afterwards in the drawing-room, when I was handing round the coffee, she had it on her finger. A little while later I believe they had another quarrel. When I went into the drawing-room to make the fire up they were sitting at opposite ends of the room, and I saw her ring on the table. I think she must have taken it off and put it there. At any rate, she walked out of the room whilst I was there, and Mr Richter followed her. I went out soon after."

"Where did she go?" asked Dob.

"She went to Mr Durand's study. Presently I saw Mr Durand and Miss May going back to the drawing-room."

"Where was Mr Richter?"

"He had gone back to the drawing-room, and whilst I was standing in the passage he came out again very excited, and asked where was the ring."

"It had disappeared, eh?"

The girl could not speak for her tears.

"They accused me," she sobbed. "Mr Richter said dreadful things. He wanted to send for the police, and have me searched, but Miss May wouldn't allow it. I went home to my mother's—she lives in Brackton—and just as I was going, I heard Mr Richter say, 'You allow her to go out of the house without searching her. It is madness.'"

Here the interview was interrupted by a sharp ring of the telephone. Dob took up the receiver, and immediately recognised May's voice.

"Have you heard about my ring?" she inquired.

"Yes." answered Dob. "The girl has come straight to me."

"I'm awfully glad," May's pleasure was not disguised. "What do you think about it, Mr Dobbly?"

"I am thinking just as you are thinking."

"What am I thinking?" she asked.

"What I am thinking," he replied evasively.

"Will you come up and see me tonight? And please tell Alice that I don't for one moment believe she stole the ring."

Dob gave the girl the message, and it brightened her up wonderfully.

"I knew Miss May wouldn't think I was a thief. The ring must have fallen on to the floor, and it is probably under the big table in the centre of the room. Do you think Mr Richter will take any action?" he asked anxiously.

"I shouldn't think so," said Dob, but here, he was mistaken.

He opened the door for the girl, to find a stranger standing in the doorway, and behind him Mr Richter.

"Ah!" cried Jacques exultantly, "I thought you'd be here. This is the girl, inspector."

The poor girl shrank back against the indignant Dob.

"You're surely not going to arrest this girl?"

"I'm afraid I must, sir," answered the inspector. "Mr Richter has made a charge and, at any rate, I shall have to question her very closely. She can either be questioned here or at the station."

"Have you a warrant? That is my point," asked Dob impatiently.

"Well, I haven't a warrant," replied the inspector, "but I have authority to detain her."

Dob looked at Jacques Richter.

"Mr Richter, if I were you I do not think I should charge Alice."

"I am going to get my ring back," responded Richter defiantly.

"Suppose I undertake to produce the ring?"

"I don't see how you can. You weren't at the house last night."

If he thought to anger Dob he was greatly mistaken.

Dob's answer was that smile of his which had so often proved wholly infectious.

"You can't charge this girl because you've no other proof than your suspicions," he explained, "and the inspector knows that as well as I. Moreover, the ring was not your property, but if anybody's, the property of Miss May Durand, and Miss Durand is perfectly convinced that the girl is innocent."

The inspector was in a dilemma.

"Do you mind if I ask the girl a few questions?"

"Fire away," granted Dob, and for half an hour the inspector plied the girl with question on question without, however, coming any nearer to the conviction that she was guilty.

Long before he was through Mr Richter had left in disgust.

"I don't see how I can even detain the girl on this evidence, sir," said the inspector, who was from Brackton, and well known to Dob. "What were you telling Mr Richter about finding the stone! You're not a private detective, are you?" he inquired, with a twinkle in his eye.

"I'm better than a private detective," answered Dob.

He called at the Durand's house that night, and was rather surprised to find Mr Richter present at an interview which he hoped would be confidential. For Dob had something on his mind, and was undecided as to how he should proceed.

Evidently, between the two young people the relationship remained strained. Dob was conscious of the tenseness of the atmosphere when he came into the room, and he stood uncomfortably, looking from one to the other.

"You asked me to come up, Miss Durand?"

She nodded.

"Really, May," protested Richter, white with anger, "I do think that you might keep this fellow out of the case. Surely it's sufficiently complicated without getting a Dud—"

"I hope you won't be rude to me," interrupted Dob suavely, "because to-night I want to keep my mind just rightly balanced, and nothing disturbs my mind so much as annoyance. Miss Durand, do you mind if I ask you a very intimate and almost unpardonably rude question?"

"I can't imagine you asking such a question," smiled the girl, "But I tell you that you may ask it."

"Do you love this man?" asked Dob, bluntly.

Mr Richter choked and the girl looked at him in wide-eyed astonishment.

"Really, Mr Dobbly," she began, a faint flush in her cheeks, "that is an extraordinary question to ask."

"It's the only question I can ask," went on Dob doggedly. "I hoped to be able to see you alone."

"I dare say you did," sneered Richter.

"I repeat, do you love this man?"

She thought for a moment, then looked him straight in the eyes.

"I tell you as frankly that I do not," and this time Mr Richter collapsed on to a chair.

"Then," continued Dob, a slow smile dawning on his face, "here is your ring."

He held out his hand, and the girl gasped, for between his forefinger and thumb glittered the pear-shaped diamond.

"How on earth—?" she cried.

"I borrowed it," explained Dob, speaking slowly, "from a gentleman who has the good fortune to own it."

She looked from him to the white-faced Richter.

"Did Jacques lend it to you! I don't understand."

"I borrowed it from its rightful owner, whose name is Abramovitch, a jeweller of Hatton Garden."

"Mr Richter sprang to his feet.

"I'm not going to sit here and listen to all this tommy-rot," and with no other word slammed out of the room.

The girl looked after him in amazement.

"Now, Mr Dobbly, perhaps you will tell me just what it all means," pleaded the girl, after he had gone.

"I can't tell you the whole of the story, Miss Durand, because I do not know what is Mr Richter's financial position. I gather, however, that it is a pretty rotten one, for inquiries I have made today show me that he is in debt on every hand."

"But how could he be in debt if he bought me a ring?"

"He didn't buy the ring at all," smiled Dob. "He borrowed it, or rather he bought it on approval! The ring belongs to a man named Abramovitch, and I had to give him a cheque for three thousand pounds before to allowed me to bring it away. Apparently Mr Richter, anticipating a much earlier marriage than you had decided, persuaded Abramovitch to let him have the ring, promising payment immediately after the marriage. When he found that the marriage had been postponed, Abramovitch demanded full settlement of his account. I had an interview with the old gentleman today, and he was very emphatic upon the point. He had put through inquiries as to Richter's financial position, and discovered that it was a pretty rotten one, and demanded that either the ring had to be paid for or returned."

"When you took the ring from your finger and left the room, Mr Richter had his opportunity. He pocketed the ring and, in order to take suspicion from himself, he was low-down enough to charge a perfectly innocent parlour-maid with having stolen it."

"But how did you know this?"

"I saw Richter and Abramovitch lunching together," explained Dob, "and after the ring had disappeared I put two and two together, and made a very startling four. This afternoon I interviewed the jeweller, and he told me the story."

She took the ring from her finger, upon which she had slipped it, and handed it to him.

"I am very glad I know," she said. "Why--" she hesitated, "why did you ask me whether I loved Jacques Richter?"

Dob cleared his throat.

"Because," he spoke a little huskily, "if you had loved him, I would not have exposed him, but would have given you back the ring without a word."

She dropped her eyes.

"Why?" she asked in a low voice.

"Because I love you too well to hurt you," answered Dob quietly.

She walked to the fireplace and stood looking into the flames. Presently, without turning her head, she said—

"What are you going to do with that ring?"

"I am returning it to Mr Abramovitch. He undertook to return any cheque, or to give me a portion of the money and get me a perfectly good engagement ring."

Again she was silent.

"What do you want an engagement ring for?" she inquired.

He stepped behind her, and put his arms round her waist, and her head dropped on his shoulder.

"That is the first silly question you have ever asked me," he replied softly.

Edgar Wallace – A Short Biography

Richard Horatio Edgar Wallace was born on the 1st April 1875 at 7 Ashburnham Grove, Greenwich. His mother, Mary Jane "Polly" Richards was born into an Irish Catholic family in Liverpool in 1843 and had worked in theatres, both as an actress in bit-parts and as a stagehand and usherette, until she married a Merchant Navy Captain, Joseph Richards, in 1867. He too had been born into an Irish Catholic family in Liverpool. His father had also been a Captain in the Merchant Navy, and his mother's family had a marine background. Mary was eight months pregnant with Joseph's child when he died at sea, and it was once the child had been born that she first turned to the stage, taking the stage name Polly Richards.

She joined the Marriott family theatre troupe in 1872. It was managed by Mrs. Alice Edgar, Richard Edgar, Grace Edgar, Adeline Edgar and Richard Horatio Edgar, Wallace's father. In late 1874 Mary and Richard Horatio Edgar had a brief sexual encounter at the party following a successful show, and she fell pregnant. Worried about the scandal which would ensue and fearing that she might forever lose her job at the troupe, she fabricated an obligation in Greenwich would detain her there for at least six months. She lived in a room in the boarding house on Ashburnham Grove until her son, Edgar, was born. She had already made preparations through her midwife for a couple to foster the child, and when Edgar was born the midwife presented her with Mrs Freeman. Her husband was a fishmonger at Billingsgate market and she already had ten children. She was happy to foster the child and for Polly to make frequent visits to see him in exchange for a small sum of money which Polly made from her work in the theatre troupe.

Wallace was now known as Richard Horatio Edgar Freeman, taking his father's forenames and his foster family's surname. Broadly speaking his childhood was a happy one. The Freemans looked after him lovingly and he had good friendships with his foster siblings, particularly Clara Freeman, twenty years his senior, who often looked after him as a child. After a few years Polly's finances tightened and she was no longer in a position to afford the fee she had been paying the Freemans. However, they had grown to love the young Wallace and opted to adopt him in order to keep him out of the workhouse. Polly could no longer visit him. George Freeman was keen to ensure that he had equal opportunities and did all he could to secure him an education at St. Alfege with St. Peter's, a Peckham boarding school. Despite his adoptive father's efforts, though, Wallace left the school aged twelve for truancy.

Instead he went to work and by the time he was fourteen or fifteen he had experience selling newspapers at Ludgate Circus, near Fleet Street, as a worker in a rubber factory, as a shoe shop assistant, as a milk delivery boy and as a ship's cook. He stole from the milk company which resulted in his dismissal, and in 1894 was engaged to a local girl from Deptford named Edith Anstree, though he broke this off and instead joined the Infantry. He adopted the name Edgar Wallace which he took from Lew Wallace, the author of *Ben-Hur*, and his medical record records a diminutive 33" chest and a stunted growth. his first posting was with the West Kent Regiment in South Africa in 1896, though he did not enjoy military life, arranging to be transferred to the Royal Army Medical Corps. Though this was a less strenuous job, it was also significantly less pleasant and so he again transferred to the Press Corps, which he found suited him far better.

He was in Cape Town in 1898 where he met Rudyard Kipling and was inspired to begin writing and publishing poetry and songs. His first collection of ballads, *The Mission that Failed!* and was enough of a success that in 1899 he paid his way out of the armed forces in order to turn to writing full time. His first work was as a war correspondent for Reuters who kept him in Africa to cover the Boer War, and then for the Daily Mail in 1900 and various other periodicals after that. It was while he was in South Africa that he met and married Ivy Maude Caldecott, who was 21 when they married in 1901, despite her Wesleyan missionary father's strong opposition to the union, for several reasons, one of which was that Wallace's writing was not turning quite the profit he had expected it would. *War and Other Poems* and *Writ in Barracks,* both published in 1900, had not proved as popular as his first collection. Eleanor Clare Hellier Wallace, their first child, died of meningitis in 1903 and, in rather deep debt, they returned to London. Wallace used his contacts with the Daily Mail to get work with them in London, electing to write detective novels as a means of making quick money.

Wallace met Polly, his birth mother, in 1903. He didn't remember her from his childhood as he had been too young when she became unable to visit, so it was as though they were meeting for the first time. She was sixty years old and terminally ill, living in abject poverty. She had come to Wallace seeking financial support, but he turned her away. She died in the Bradford Infirmary later that year. In 1904 he and Ivy had a son, Bryan. He was still writing and had completed his first thriller, *The Four Just Men*. Since nobody would publish it he resorted to setting up his own publishing company which he called Tallis Press and he published a serialised version of *The Four Just Men* in 1905. He received promotional assistance from the Daily Mail in which he ran a competition for entrants to guess the method of murder in the final chapter, with a prize of £1,000 for a correct guess. Although the paper's proprietor, Lord Alfred Harmsworth, refused Wallace the £1,000 prize money, Wallace persisted and went ahead with the competition, recklessly advertising on billboards and buses all over the country, hoping to expand his advertisements across the Empire. His worried colleagues at the Daily Mail managed to convince him to lower the prize money to £500, split into a first prize of £250, a second prize of £200 and a third of £50, but with the total cost of his advertisements nearing £2,000 he would need to sell £2,500 worth of copies before he could see any profit. He was confident that this could be achieved in just three months.

Though he had remarkable enthusiasm, it became clear that his managerial skills left a lot to be desired. It soon emerged that nowhere in the competition terms and conditions had he included a clause limiting the competition to one single winner; instead, any entrant with a winning answer was entitled to their corresponding prize money. Thus, if ten entrants guessed the first prize answer, the competition was obliged to pay each entrant £250. This error was only noticed after the competition had been closed and the solution had been printed in the final installment of the novel, meaning that not only was there no opportunity to write his way out of enormous financial obligation, but the entrants who had guessed correctly would by now have read the final chapter and know they had done so. £250 was an enormous amount of money to the average Edwardian family and those entitled to it were likely to make a lot of noise if they didn't receive their money. Despite this, Wallace's fist instinct was to attempt to ignore the issue entirely, even as he discovered that he initial calculations had been dramatically over-enthusiastic and it would take nearer to two years of continuous sales to break even at the initial cost of £2,500, let alone the new figure which included every correct guesser. Compounding the problem even further was the awful realisation that as sales continued throughout the initial three month period and Wallace approached the £2,500 break-even figure, new readers were still eligible to enter and guess correctly. Though it is unknown how much he eventually owed his readers, Lord Harmsworth found himself having to loan over £5,000 in order to protect the reputation of the newspaper, since 1906 had come around and there still hadn't been a list printed of all prize-winners. It was less a charitable act than one of a man anxious that the failure would reflect ill on his own paper. Wallace filed for bankruptcy shortly thereafter and as a token gesture to his creditors sold the rights to the novel to Sir George Newnes, a publisher and editor, for £75. In the midst of this chaos though, Wallace managed to write and published *Smithy*, which would become the first of a series of *Smithy* novels.

Following this fiascos Wallace was dismissed from the Daily Mail in 1907 when inaccuracies which were found in his reporting, resulting in libel cases being brought against the paper. That year he became the first reporter to be fired from the Daily Mail and was his awful reputation prevented him from finding work at any other papers. Despite all this, though, he travelled to the Congo Free State later that year and reported on the criminal treatment of the Congolese people by King Leopold II of Belgium and the Belgian rubber companies. Up to fifteen million Congolese were killed in various atrocities, and Wallace was asked to serialise stories based on his experiences for her penny magazine *Weekly Tale-Teller*. He and Ivy had another daughter, named Patricia, in 1908. Though his new work for *Weekly Tale-Teller* was bringing in some money, their financial situation was still dire and Ivy was occasionally forced to sell off her jewellery and possessions in order to pay for food. In 1911 his Congolese stories were published in a collection called *Sanders of the River*, which quickly became a bestseller. He would publish eleven more such collections featuring a total of 102 stories of adventure and tribal life set on the river Congo.

From 1908 he started to enjoy a revival of both his success and his reputation. The majority of his initial writing he sold outright in order to make money as quickly as possible and placate his creditors in the United Kingdom and South Africa, but as his success saw the reestablishment of his reputation he began to find work once again as a journalist, beginning in horse racing for the *Week-End*, the *Evening News* and then as an editor for the *Week-End Racing Supplement*. Following this success he started his own racing papers, *Bibury's* and *R. E. Walton's Weekly*, eventually buying his own racehorses and losing thousands gambling. His success was insufficient to support his newly extravagant lifestyle and his marriage began to fail in the light of his financial irresponsibility. He and Ivy had their last child together, Michael Blair Wallace, in 1916, and she filed for divorce in 1918 moving to Tunbridge Wells with her children.

Wallace began to fall for his secretary Ethel Violet King and they married in 1921, having a child, Penelope Wallace, in 1923, who would herself go on to become a successful crime writer. Wallace now began to take his career as a fiction writer more seriously, signing with Hodder and Stoughton in 1921. He now began to organize his contracts more carefully, arranging for royalties and properly organized promotions, run by people more business-minded than himself. He was marketed as the 'King of Thrillers' and they gave him the trademark image of a trilby, a cigarette holder and a yellow Rolls Royce.

He was truly prolific, capable not only of producing a 70,000 word novel in three days but of doing three novels in a row in such a manner. His publishers signed off on almost everything he wrote as soon as he turned it in, estimating that by 1928 one in four books being read at any time was written by Wallace, for alongside his famous thrillers he wrote variously in other genres, including but not limited to science fiction, non-fiction accounts of WWI which amounted to ten volumes and screen plays. Eventually he would reach the remarkable total of 170 novels, 18 stage plays and 957 short stories.

Wallace became chairman of the Press Club which to this day holds an annual Edgar Wallace Award, rewarding 'excellence in writing'. In 1923 he broadcasted a report on the Epsom Derby horse race for the British Broadcasting Company, making him the first ever radio sports correspondent. His ex-wife Ivy had suffered from breast cancer between 1923-1924, and it eventually killed her in 1926 despite a successful operation to remove a tumour the year before. He wrote the essay "The Canker in our Midst" in 1926 which dealt, aggressively and controversially, with the problem of paedophilia in show business, describing how children were unwittingly left open to sexual abuse, and linking paedophilia with homosexuality. Its tone has been described as "intolerant, blustering, kick-the-blighters-down-the-stairs". He was appointed chairman of the British Lion Film Corporation on the back of the success of *The Ringer* and on the agreement that he give British Lion first choice on all his future work. This contract gave him an annual salary and a large amount of stock with the company, along with a stipend on all British Lion production of his work and 10% of their annual profits. This extraordinary contract gave him annual earnings by 1929 of almost £50,000, or almost £2 million in 2014.

He now became an active figure in politics, entering the 1931 general election as a Liberal contestant in Blackpool, rejecting the current government in favour of free trade. He lost the election by over 33,000 votes and went to America in late 1931, once again deeply in debt after buying the *Sunday News* which closed six months later. In America he quickly found work as a script doctor for RKO Pictures, enjoying early success with the 1932 adaptation of *The Hound of the Baskervilles*. This success, along with that of the play *The Green Pack*, established his reputation in America and he was able to see his own work adapted for film, beginning with *The Four Just Men*. His most successful theatrical work, *On The Spot*, which explores the life of Al Capone, has been described as "arguably, in construction, dialogue, action, plot and resolution, still one of the finest and purest of 20th-century melodramas". These successes led to his assignation on RKO's "gorilla picture" which would become famous as King Kong in 1933.

He worked on the first draft though he was beginning to experience severe headaches which brought about a diagnosis of diabetes. Despite taking medication to address his condition, it deteriorated in a matter of days. His wife booked him passage home but soon heard that he had entered a coma and died of his condition and double pneumonia on the 7th of February 1932 in North Maple Drive, Beverly Hills. In his honour the bell at St. Bride's church on Fleet Street tolled for the duration of the morning while the flags flew at half-mast. He was buried near his home in England at Chalklands, Bourne End, in Buckinghamshire. Once again, at the time of his death he was in severe debt, mostly to racing bookkeepers, though these debts were settled within two years thanks to the enormous royalties his estate continued to receive from his contracts. His writing has been translated into 29 languages, and is considered one of the most important bodies of Colonial writing.

Edgar Wallace – A Concise Bibliography

African Novels
Sanders of the River (1911)

The People of the River (1911)
The River of Stars (1913)
Bosambo of the River (1914)
Bones (1915)
The Keepers of the King's Peace (1917)
Lieutenant Bones (1918)
Bones in London (1921)
Sandi the Kingmaker (1922)
Bones of the River (1923)
Sanders (1926)
Again Sanders (1928)

Four Just Men (Series)
The Four Just Men (1905)
The Council of Justice (1908)
The Just Men of Cordova (1917)
The Law of the Four Just Men (US title: Again the Three Just Men) (1921)
The Three Just Men (1926)
Again the Three Just Men (US title: The Law of the Three Just Men) (1929) a.k.a. Again the Three

Mr. J. G. Reeder (Series)
Room 13 (1924)
The Mind of Mr. J. G. Reeder (US title: The Murder Book of Mr. J. G. Reeder) (1925)
Terror Keep (1927)
Red Aces (1929)
The Guv'nor and Other Short Stories (US title: Mr. Reeder Returns) (1932)

Detective Sgt. (Inspector) Elk series
The Nine Bears or The Other Man or The Cheaters (1910)
revised as Silinski - Master Criminal (1930)
The Fellowship of the Frog (1925)
The Joker or The Colossus (1926)
The Twister (1928)
The India-Rubber Men (1929)
White Face (1930)

Educated Evans (Series)
Educated Evans (1924)
More Educated Evans (1926)
Good Evans (1927)

Smithy (Series)
Smithy (1905)
Smithy Abroad (1909)
Smithy and The Hun (1915)
Nobby or Smithy's Friend Nobby (1916)

Crime Novels

Angel Esquire (1908)
The Fourth Plague or Red Hand (1913)
Grey Timothy or Pallard the Punter (1913)
The Man Who Bought London (1915)
The Melody of Death (1915)
A Debt Discharged (1916)
The Tomb of T'Sin (1916)
The Secret House (1917)
The Clue of the Twisted Candle (1918)
Down under Donovan (1918)
The Man Who Knew (1918)
The Strange Lapses of Larry Loman (1918)
The Green Rust (1919)
Kate Plus Ten (1919)
The Daffodil Mystery or The Daffodil Murder (1920)
Jack O' Judgment (1920)
The Angel of Terror or The Destroying Angel (1922)
The Crimson Circle (1922)
Mr. Justice Maxwell or Take-A-Chance Anderson (1922)
The Valley of Ghosts (1922)
Captains of Souls (1923)
The Clue of the New Pin (1923)
The Green Archer (1923)
The Missing Million (1923)
The Dark Eyes of London or The Croakers (1924)
Double Dan or Diana of Kara-Kara (US Title) (1924)
The Face in the Night or The Diamond Men or The Ragged Princess (1924)
The Sinister Man (1924)
The Three Oak Mystery (1924)
The Blue Hand or Beyond Recall (1925)
The Daughters of the Night (1925)
The Gaunt Stranger or Police Work (1925) revised as The Ringer (1926)
A King by Night (1925)
The Strange Countess (1925)
The Avenger or The Hairy Arm (1926)
The Black Abbot (1926)
The Day of Uniting (1926)
The Door with Seven Locks (1926)
The Man from Morocco or Souls In Shadows or The Black (US Title) (1926)
The Million Dollar Story (1926)
The Northing Tramp or The Tramp (1926)
Penelope of the Polyantha (1926)
The Square Emerald or The Woman (1926)
The Terrible People or The Gallows' Hand (1926)
We Shall See! or The Gaol-Breakers (US Title) (1926)
The Yellow Snake or The Black Tenth (1926)
Big Foot (1927)
The Feathered Serpent or Inspector Wade or Inspector Wade and the Feathered Serpent (1927)

Flat 2 (1927)
The Forger or The Counterfeiter (1927)
Terror Keep (1927)
The Hand of Power or The Proud Sons of Ragusa (1927)
The Man Who Was Nobody (1927)
Number Six (1927)
The Squeaker or The Sign of the Leopard or The Squealer (US Title) (1927)
The Traitor's Gate (1927)
The Double (1928)
The Flying Squad (1928)
The Gunner or Gunman's Bluff (US Title) (1928)
Four Square Jane or The Fourth Square (1929)
The Golden Hades or Stamped In Gold or The Sinister Yellow Sign (1929)
The Green Ribbon (1929)
The Calendar (1930)
The Clue of the Silver Key or The Silver Key (1930)
The Lady of Ascot (1930)
The Devil Man or Sinister Street or Silver Steel
or The Life and Death of Charles Peace (1931)
The Man at the Carlton or The Mystery of Mary Grier (1931)
The Coat of Arms or The Arranways Mystery (1931)
On the Spot: Violence and Murder in Chicago (1931)
When the Gangs Came to London or Scotland Yard's Yankee Dick
or The Gangsters Come To London (1932)
The Frightened Lady or The Case of the Frightened Lady or Criminal At Large (1933)
The Green Pack (1933)
The Man Who Changed His Name (1935)
The Mouthpiece (1935)
Smoky Cell (1935)
The Table (1936)
Sanctuary Island (1936)

Other Novels
Captain Tatham of Tatham Island or Eve's Island or The Island of Galloping Gold (1909)
The Duke in the Suburbs (1909)
Private Selby (1912)
1925 - The Story of a Fatal Peace (1915)
Those Folk of Bulboro (1918)
The Book of all Power (1921)
Flying Fifty-five (1922)
The Books of Bart (1923)
Barbara on Her Own (1926)

Poetry Collections
The Mission That Failed (1898)
War and Other Poems (1900)
Writ In Barracks (1900)

Non-Fiction

Unofficial Despatches of the Anglo-Boer War (1901)
Famous Scottish Regiments (1914)
Field Marshal Sir John French (1914)
Heroes All: Gallant Deeds of the War (1914)
The Standard History of the War – Volumes 1 – 4 (1914)
Kitchener's Army and the Territorial Forces:
The Full Story of a Great Achievement (1915)
Vol. 2-4. War of the Nations (1915)
Vol. 5-7. War of the Nations (1916)
Vol. 8-9. War of the Nations (1917)
Famous Men and Battles of the British Empire (1917)
Tam of the Scouts (1918)
The Real Shell-Man: The Story of Chetwynd of Chilwell (1919)
People or Edgar Wallace by Himself (1926)
The Trial of Patrick Herbert Mahon (1928)
My Hollywood Diary (1932)

Screenplays

King Kong (1932, first draft of original screenplay, 110 pages) While the script was not used in its
entirety, much of it was retained for the final screenplay.
The Hound of the Baskervilles (1932, British film)
The Squeaker (1930, British film)
Prince Gabby (1929, British film)
Mark of the Frog (1928, American film)
The Valley of Ghosts (192

Short Story Collections

The Admirable Carfew (1914)
The Adventure of Heine (1917)
Tam O' the Scouts (1918)
The Fighting Scouts (1919)
Chick (1923)
The Black Avons (1925)
The Brigand (1927)
The Mixer (1927)
This England (1927)
The Orator (1928)
The Thief in the Night (1928)
Elegant Edward (1928)
The Lone House Mystery and Other Stories (1929)
The Governor of Chi-Foo (1929)
Again the Ringer The Ringer Returns (US Title) (1929)
The Big Four or Crooks of Society (1929)
The Black or Blackmailers I Have Foiled (1929)
The Cat-Burglar (1929)
Circumstantial Evidence (1929)
Fighting Snub Reilly (1929)

For Information Received (1929)
Forty-Eight Short Stories (1929)
Planetoid 127 and The Sweizer Pump (1929)
The Ghost of Down Hill & The Queen of Sheba's Belt (1929)
The Iron Grip (1929)
The Lady of Little Hell (1929)
The Little Green Man (1929)
The Prison-Breakers (1929)
The Reporter (1929)
Killer Kay (1930)
Mrs William Jones and Bill (1930)
Forty Eight Short Stories (George Newnes Limited ca. 1930)
The Stretelli Case and Other Mystery Stories (1930)
The Terror (1930)
The Lady Called Nita (1930)
Sergeant Sir Peter or Sergeant Dunn, C.I.D. (1932)
The Scotland Yard Book of Edgar Wallace (1932)
The Steward (1932)
Nig-Nog and other humorous stories (1934)
The Last Adventure (1934)
The Woman From the East (1934) Co-written By Robert George Curtis
The Edgar Wallace Reader of Mystery and Adventure (1943)
The Undisclosed Client (1963)

Other
King Kong, with Draycott M. Dell, (1933), 28 October 1933 Cinema Weekly

Plays
An African Millionaire (1904)
The Forest of Happy Dreams (1910)
Dolly Cutting Herself (1911)
The Manager's Dream (1914)
M'Lady (1921)
Double Dan (1926)
The Mystery of room 45 (1926)
A Perfect Gentleman (1927)
The Terror (1927)
Traitors Gate (1927)
The Lad (1928)
The Man Who Changed His Name (1928)
The Squeaker (1928)
The Calendar (1929)
Persons Unknown (1929)
The Ringer (1929)
The Mouthpiece (1930)
On the Spot (1930)
Smoky Cell (1930)
The Squeaker (1930)

To Oblige A Lady (1930)
The Case of the Frightened Lady (1931)
The Old Man (1931)
The Green Pack (1932)
The Table (1932)